CW00890219

Bounty Gun

BOUNTY GUN

LUTHER CHANCE

A Black Horse Western

ROBERT HALE • LONDON

ISBN 0 7090 6008 4

Robert Hale Limited
Clerkenwell House
Clerkenwell Green
London EC1R 0HT

Typeset in Palatino by
Pitfold Design, Hindhead, Surrey.
Printed and bound in Great Britain by
WBC Book Manufacturers Limited,
Bridgend, Mid-Glamorgan.

*This one
for L. and P. as
they settle to
the homestead*

ONE

The man sprawled helpless in the hot sand like a flayed lizard and waited for the next vicious kick to settle somewhere in his back. It came with a sickening thud, burying the rough-edged toe of a boot deep into his ribs. He squirmed, groaned, clawed at the empty sand and blinked through blood-soaked eyes on the shimmer of the day.

How much more could he take? How much more did the sonsofbitches circling him want? His death, as slow and agonizing as they could make it? Maybe they were wondering just how long it would take to kill a man without plugging him full of hot lead. Right now he would settle for the lead.

Another kick thudded into his thigh. A heel pressed into his neck. He retched, vomited, sucked dirt into his throat and began to choke on a surge of blood that ran from the gash in his head to his mouth. If death had a flavour, this had to be it. He was going to die tasting it.

'He ain't stopped breathin' yet, Clant,' piped a voice. 'Not yet he ain't.'

'Then yuh ain't tryin',' drawled the answer.

'Sure I am,' piped the voice again. 'Must have a hide like a hog.'

'Hell, Stick, yuh beginnin' to sweat,' droned a third voice. 'I ain't seen yuh sweatin' like that since yuh chased that young whore back at Sinn Flats. And yuh didn't get nowheres with her, either!'

'Yuh just shut yuh mouth, Loose,' snapped Stick Grieves. He levelled another kick into the man's side and stood back to mop his brow. 'I swear this critter's all hide.'

Clant Warre threw a stone into the air and aimed a fount of spittle across its flight. 'Yuh either finish the fella now or leave him,' he drawled. 'We got some miles to eat up before noon.' The stone fell wet and black to the sand and dried instantly.

'I say we leave him,' said Loose Carne, kicking sand. 'He ain't goin' no place in that condition. He'll be crow meat come sundown.'

'Don't fuss me none either way,' mouthed Warre, hawking more spittle. 'Fella should've stayed clear of us. He didn't, and I ain't havin'' no nosyin' drifter tellin' on where he seen us, so I reckon yuh could say he's had a bad day. Yuh get days like that.'

'Well?' asked Carne, squinting at Grieves. 'So what yuh goin' to do? Yuh all done, or do yuh want me to clean my barrels through?'

'I'd sure like to know who he is,' said Grieves, still mopping at sweat. 'And what the hell's he doin' out here anyhow?'

'Don't reckon on him bein' a deal talkative right now,' drawled Warre. 'Yuh kinda upset him, ain't yuh?'

'I say we leave him,' snapped Carne. 'I ain't wastin' good lead on a dyin' man.'

'OK,' said Grieves. 'We leave him. Where's his horse?'

'Took off to the bush. Take what yuh want from the critter – them nice lookin' Colts for a start, and his boots. He won't be needin' either.' Clant Warre strolled to the body and spat into the man's back. 'Sure hope he looks a deal tidier time he reaches his Maker,' he drawled.

And so it was on that heat-filled day in a silent land where nothing moved that Clant Warre, Stick Grieves and Loose Carne rode due north from the place where they had half-killed and left for dead a man they had never seen before, whose name they never heard. He would be forgotten in their lives long before the last of the day's light, and they did not believe in ghosts.

Not then.

TWO

The man reached water at dusk. Cool, fresh water that trickled through the rock-bed from the distant hill range to keep alive the scant brush of the creek – and save the lives of those who might be dragged there.

Mid-afternoon had come and gone with the long shadows thickening when the man left for dead had stirred. His eyes had worked open through the sticky haze of drying blood, his fingers flexed like insects waking from siesta, but it had been another hour before a limb had moved and the man able to roll to his side.

His body burned with a ceaseless throb of pain; what did not throb only ached in the dull numbness of bruising; what did not ache was scorched with soreness. There was nothing of him that did not protest. But he was alive, breathing through a gurgling wheeze, and conscious enough in those first minutes to feel the anger knotted deep in his guts. Real anger – but real guts.

It had been the soft snort of his mount, a strawberry roan mare, that had cleared his jumbled thinking just long enough to stir the new, demanding pain of thirst. Hell, he needed water! By any means, at any price, through any effort. And soon.

The mare had moved closer, lowered her head as if to nuzzle at the heap of blood-soaked flotsam, and let the reins drift from her like tendrils. The man's reach for them had been instinctive, his fingers trembling in their grip. He had a hold, weak and tentative, but there and fixed as the mare backed, turned and began to drag him from the sand to where it filtered into loose dirt and grit and slid away to the creek bed.

He could hear the water's trickle a good half-hour before he reached it. Hear it like a voice that summoned gently and tortured in its laughter.

He had sprawled there, the cool flow splashing at his cheeks, seeping through his shirt to sting his flesh, as if content to stay forever. And why not? He might still die anyway when whatever passed for sleep in his condition finally flooded over him.

But sleep did not come with the lengthening shadows; nothing like it, as slowly, thunderously his thoughts took shape, slipped into sequence, pounded at the back of his head, throbbed in his temples and flashed into vivid images of recall.

Three faces. Three men. Stick Grieves, Clant Warre, Loose Carne . . . .

Grieves was the tall, lean, sprig of a youth with the boyish face and piping voice, and the eyes of a killer. Warre, the bulky, heavy-bellied brains of the trio with a taste for fast shooting and quick dying. Carne, the mindless drifter who followed wherever looting, ready dollars, rape and death beckoned.

Three men on the far side of Hell.

But the man had known them, trailed them for months from the southern territories to the deep Midwest for the price on their heads, the bounty that would pay his way to the planned new life in Nevada. Trailed them until this day, this place, when they had outsmarted him, jumped him, taken him completely by surprise for the first time ever. And almost succeeded in killing him – save that they had failed to find out who he was, why he was there, and finish him. A mistake, he resolved, as he sprawled in the trickle of the creek bed with the night shadows closing like a curtain, that was worth staying alive for. Tomorrow was just beginning.

*　　*　　*

But it was another full day before the man was able to move from the creek, and only then with shuffling steps through the throb of dull pain that seemed to have gripped every muscle in his body and turned his head to a spinning spur.

It took time, achingly slow time, for him to take stock of what he had left: the mare, still saddled up, complete with bedroll, panniers, canteen and, first priority as he saw it then, his prized Winchester sheathed tight in its scabbard. Thank the Lord the mare had taken to the brush!

He had his hat, his shirt, his pants, but the sonsofbitches had helped themselves to his twin Colts, belt and holsters, and, goddammit, his boots. Best fitting boots he had ever owned at that! Even so, he reckoned he stood on the credit side – and he was alive and able to ride. Or maybe he would be able to ride, and winced at the thought of mounting up.

The day had cleared to a high blue sky and the air already thickened on the prospect of the noon heat, when the man reined the mare to the north and left her to pick her own way out of the creek bed towards the bluff ahead. She needed no telling to take it easy, but no encouragement either to clear that place where the blood still stained the sand and stones.

There was no certain reckoning on where

Clant Warre might be leading his sidekicks, save that due west was empty plains country for a hundred miles with few easy pickings for the likes of the trio.

Due south offered only desert; the east too many towns where Warre was top of the wanted list. Which left the north. Hill country, pine forests, long hidden gulches, tight valleys, homesteads, and at least three shanty towns. That seemed more like Warre's choice of territory, the man figured, especially through a long, hot summer. Due north would appeal come the Fall.

But Clant Warre would not be seeing the Fall, the man smiled. Not this Fall, not any Fall. Winter, cold and dead, would come early this year . . . .

The mare had eased into her first steady canter of the day as she carried her slumped, half-asleep rider to the head of a slope that would drift to a valley, when the crack of gunfire split the still, sultry air and brought the man bolt upright.

More shots, fired high and loose, then the thunderous beat of hoofs, the groaning creaks of a wagon rolling at high speed – and the man was suddenly wide awake, the blood tingling to his nerve-ends for the first time in days.

THREE

A swirling cloud of dust, the vague, blurred shapes of horses at full stretch ahead of a tumbling, skidding wagon, its driver lost in the flash of movement, and behind the wagon, closing with every booming crash of their mounts' hoofs, two riders intent on only one thing.

And hell, thought the man, as he topped the slope and stared into the valley, they were going to make it!

The leading rider fired again, high, ranging shots designed to spook the wagon horses into still wilder effort as they raced blindly over the trail. The second rider whooped and shouted at the top of his voice to send echoes swaying through the hills like the laughter of ghosts. Guns flashed and spat again, the yelling grew louder, but now the riders were content to hold to the flanks of the wagon as it scudded, bounced and slid out of the driver's control towards the teeth of an outcrop of rocks that would gnash it to matchwood in seconds.

The man's mount bucked and snorted as if in anticipation of the disaster that loomed, steadied at the tightening of reins, and moved off down the treacherous, loose-rock slope to the valley floor with shuffling steps.

There was nothing the man could do now to help save the wagon, but he sure as hell intended to be there when it crunched to its dreadful fate.

The crash came like an eerie crack of lightning through the sun-swamped day. The wagon bounced, lifted, seemed to grow on the light as if it would soar to the sky. Wheels spun in wild frenzy, clamouring on the useless void of air. The horses threatened to fall, pawed crazily for their balance and broke free as the front of the wagon crashed back to the rocks and was suddenly a thousand pieces of scattered timber.

There was a single croaking scream as the driver was hurled clear of the flying debris to sprawl motionless in a swirl of shimmering dirt.

The riders closed in without pausing, sharp-eyed as hungry vultures.

The man reined the mare to a halt at the foot of the slope, cleared the sweat from his thudding brow, and narrowed his gaze on the riders. One had already dismounted, kicked aside the splinters of timber and reached the body where he squatted over it.

'Alive?' called the second rider, slithering his mount to a halt at the outcrop.

'Alive, sure enough. She'll do real nice.'

She? A woman? frowned the man, tightening his grip on the reins. He eased forward in the saddle, winced at the bite of the stirrups on his stockinged feet, patted the mare's neck, and slid the Winchester from its scabbard.

Then he came on.

The heat of the day burned in a high haze. The air rushed warm and thick at the man's face as he came at a steady pace from the foothills, his gaze tight and cold, the mare tossing her head, nostrils flared, tack jangling rhythmically to the creak of leather. Sunlight glinted on the barrel of the rifle, but the men at the body seemed neither to see or hear the approaching rider. Their concentration stayed firmly on the figure at their feet – a woman without any doubt, thought the man, catching his first glimpse of her long yellow hair as she was dragged towards a line of scrub. No doubt either why the men had been running her down, or what they planned.

But how come, he wondered, that she was out

here alone, and who were the scum about to rape her?

The man waited another half-minute before letting loose a roar of lead that broke the haze like a venomous spit. The shot kicked dirt at the men's boots and spun them from the woman as if tugged on a string. There was a look of disbelief on their sweating faces, a dazed brightening of their eyes, seconds when they seemed fixed and immobile in the shimmering land.

Then, almost as one, they reached for their Colts.

The man had released the reins and given the mare a freedom she responded to without asking as the Winchester was raised, levelled, steadied. The recoil shuddered into his shoulder, lifting the familiar pain he had felt at the feet of Stick Grieves. There was a tumbling surge of sweat across the man's brow, a stifled moan from deep within him, but the shots ripped into their targets with the sting of a rattler's strike.

One man was thrown from his feet, his hand still on the butt of his gun, and tossed into the scrub as if a discarded scrap of meat. The second stood his ground for breathless, gurgling moments, his fingers clawing aimlessly at his blood-soaked gut. He raised his eyes in a slow, haunted gaze to the phantom from the hills that circled him, and felt death hugging like a fever, then fell face down and twitched only once in the scorching dirt.

The mare snorted, the man merely grunted and slid the Winchester home to its scabbard.

It took more than an hour for the man to rig a primitive shade for the woman, himself and the mare from blankets dragged from the wagon wreckage; to help himself to a pair of boots from the feet of the taller of the two dead bodies, the belt, holsters and Colts from the thicker-set fellow; to round-up the riders' mounts and hitch them, take stock of the water to hand and dampen the woman's brow and lips. She was breathing, sure enough, but hell she looked rough, too rough to move, he decided. Nothing for it but to wait. She would come to in good time.

Meanwhile . . . . His body throbbed, his head was spinning, his eyes glazing with the demands of sleep. Meanwhile. . . . Maybe the critters he had shot had been lone drifters. But somewhere up ahead Clant Warre and his sidekicks were riding free.

The thought was still troubling him when his eyes finally closed.

FOUR

She was in her late twenties, edging thirty; handsome too, with clean-cut features, a delicate mouth, but a fiercely determined chin; long yellow hair, and a figure, he reckoned, that would turn many an eager head. A fellow would be proud to be seen with this woman, thought the man, especially when she was dressed real good and not looking as she did right now as if she had been on a three-months' trail drive. She would not be wanting then for close company, he figured.

So how come she had been driving a wagon alone and out here through wild Midwestern country? And why?

She had stirred only once in the last hour, soon after the man himself had woken from a fretful sleep, his head and body still throbbing. Her eyes had opened, blue and misty, and for a moment there had been a jolt of fear, a shudder, a bewildered look clouding her face, until the man had calmed her with a quiet word and gentle touch and she had lapsed back into whatever crowded her sleep. If sleep it really was.

The man had rummaged through the scattered contents of the wagon in the hope of finding something that would identify the woman, or maybe give a clue as to where she had come from and where she was heading. But there had been nothing save clothing, a few personal belongings, bedding, pots and pans, a rocking chair, dressing-table. Looked as if the woman had packed up wherever home had been and simply left. He wondered why.

The bodies of the two men who had attacked the wagon had yielded exactly what the man had expected: the trappings, filth and stink of roughneck drifters. So where and when had they come on the scene? And how many more of them were there?

The man had shrugged and gone back to the shade to ponder his next move. The woman would have to be tended to, that was for sure. He would have to get her to some town or at least a friendly homestead where she could recover in peace and safety. That done he would need to hit the trail north again and try to pick up the tracks of Clant Warre. Sonofabitch had a three-day start on him and could be riding fast for whatever damnation he had a mind for. Or maybe he had slipped clear of the northern trail and turned west. Could be weeks, maybe months before he surfaced again.

The man had shifted his body impatiently, winced at the aches and stabs of pain, and gazed at the sleeping woman. Time she stirred. Time she gave him a name and told her sorry tale.

But it was still some time into the afternoon before the woman was fully awake, on her feet, and had summoned the courage to venture from the makeshift shade to watch the man where he tended the horses. It took almost as long for her watchful gaze to settle and for her to speak without coming too close.

'This your doin', mister?' she asked, flicking her eyes to the bodies of the wagon raiders. 'You kill them?'

''Fraid so, ma'am,' said the man, as he tightened the hitch-line. 'But I figure they had it comin', anyhow.'

The woman tidied her hair nervously. 'I didn't hear you,' she began again. 'Didn't even see you.'

'No, ma'am, yuh didn't at that. Yuh were a mite preoccupied at the time, as I recall. Yuh feelin' better now?'

'Much, thank you.' She hesitated. 'Guess I owe you some – for this.' She gestured to the bodies. 'Don't reckon they had it in mind to be neighbourly.'

'Nothin' like it, ma'am, not from where I was watchin'.' The man turned from the line. 'I'll cover 'em before we leave. Sorry about yuh wagon. Couldn't do much about that.'

The woman's gaze moved over the wreckage. 'Seems like there ain't a deal left worth collecting.' She took a deep breath. 'Not that there was much to begin with.'

'Care to tell me about it, ma'am?' asked the man, carefully.

'Yuh that bothered?'

'I got bothered some hours back, ma'am,' he smiled gently.

The woman tossed her long hair. 'Of course,' she murmured. 'I'm sorry. I owe you an explanation.'

'A name would be a starter.'

'Mary Jo Goldway.'

The man grunted and tipped the brim of his hat. 'Pleased to meet you Miss Goldway.'

'It might be Mrs Goldway,' she said sharply.

'It might,' grinned the man, 'but it ain't. Yuh ain't wearin' no weddin' ring. I noticed.'

The woman lowered her gaze and smiled to herself. 'Naturally.' She waited a moment, scuffing the toe of her boot into sand. 'I lived with my Pa back east, just short of Willadon. We had a spread there – cattle horses – ran the place ourselves with a couple of hired hands. But Pa died five months back. I couldn't handle the place myself, so I sold up and — ' She paused as if examining the scuffs in the sand. 'Decided to move on. Simple as that.'

'Alone?' frowned the man. 'This far west?'

The woman tossed her hair again. 'Reckoned I could cope. Always have – until today.' She shrugged. 'Just bad luck crossin' the trail of them scum.'

'Close to *real* bad luck, ma'am!'

The woman's stare tightened. 'You don't have to spell it out, mister. I know what might have happened, and I'm grateful to you it didn't. Said as much.' She paused again. 'You got a name?'

The man's eyes narrowed. 'Maguire, ma'am. Just Maguire. That'll do.'

'Well, Mister Maguire, like I say I'm grateful to you, and just as soon I can collect what's worth savin' here, I'll be movin' on. Perhaps we can ride together for as long as it suits. Company would be welcome.'

'Sure, ma'am,' said the man, easing the sweat from his hatband. 'Be my pleasure, but I don't exactly figure yuh thinkin'. This ain't no sorta country for a woman trailin' alone. And it gets a whole lot worse. Yuh seen somethin' of the critters foulin' it, and they weren't by no means the meanest. They get meaner, 'specially where women are concerned – and 'specially where a woman on her own happens across them. So I'd reckon yuh got to have one helluva good reason for goin' on. One helluva good reason.'

The woman stiffened, stood tall, her chin defiant. 'I have,' she said. 'A very good reason to my thinkin'.'

The man waited. 'Tell me,' he murmured.

'Last thing my Pa asked before he died was that I'd go find his brother. He hadn't seen him in twenty years, and he wanted me to make sure he was alive and well. Said as how he'd changed his name from Goldway way back, but Pa was sure the fella was out here, somewhere in the Midwest. Promised him I would. And I will – whatever it takes.'

'And just who is this long-lost brother?' asked the man. 'He gotta name?'

'Sure he has. Fella's name – my uncle's name – is now Warre. Clant Warre.'

FIVE

The valley had filled with a brood of early shadows. The wagon wreckage lay like black bones, the leftovers of the raid, and the place had filled with a strange, listening silence broken only by the scuff of hoofs, jangle of tack and creak of leather as Maguire, Mary Jo Goldway and their trailed mounts made a slow track into the foothills and the beckoning dusk.

But it might as well have been the depths of night for Maguire.

Damn it, the whole darned situation was impossible! A fantasy, a nightmare, some sweating hell that would fade when he woke – save that he *was* awake, wide awake, and this was no fantasy. But it was a living nightmare.

How was it, he wondered, his gaze blind to the reaching slopes of the hills, that in all this country, the hundreds of miles of the sprawl of it, that he should be the one – darn it, the only one! – to meet up with Clant Warre's niece? How come the fates had dealt him, the man intent on hunting the sonofabitch to his death, the bounty hunter planning on making Warre and his sidekicks his final prize, this ridiculous hand? And how in hell was he supposed to play it?

He had somehow stifled his shock at the woman's announcement and what she intended, but it had turned like a cold stone in his guts. No doubt about it, Mary Jo Goldway was determined enough to trail forth in search of her uncle as a promise to her pa, and just as innocent of the true identity of Warre, his way of life, what he had become and stood for in this wild country. So maybe he should tell her right now; come straight out with it and send her packing back east.

Would it be that easy?

Would he have the courage to tell her of how Warre and his scum had beaten him near senseless not three days ago, that there was a price on the fellow's head, dead or alive, and that he, Maguire, was planning to collect?

Should he tell her to stay close and that sooner or later he would lead her to Warre and she could watch while he shot her uncle before her eyes? Could he then turn when it was done and tell her that the sonofabitch had it coming anyhow, retribution for all his killing, looting, raping and robbing? Would that be the way of it?

Hell!

Or could he in some way, by some means, get rid of Mary Jo Goldway?

Maybe he could play along with her for a day or so, get her to some town, then send her off on a fool's chase on the lie that Warre had been seen south, west, any darned where! Maybe she would buy it. And maybe it would be that she would never find her uncle, or even hear of him, leastways not until he was long dead and furnishing some remote Boot Hill.

Hell!

Could he do that? Would he? Or had the fates already planned it otherwise, in some other place, some other time?

Hell!

'We goin' to settle some place for the night, Mister Maguire?' called the woman at his back.

'Sure,' he answered. 'Up there, at the tree line.'

Maybe now would be the chance to shake her off, ride on deep into the night, be miles away come sun-up, free to hunt down Clant Warre and kill him as he wanted, in his own good time.

'Hell!' he murmured as he reined his mount to the trees.

She looked calmer in the glow of the firelight, more relaxed, with a deal more colour to her cheeks, a brighter sparkle in her eyes. She would sleep easy tonight, thought Maguire as he watched her. Which was a whole lot more than could be said for his prospects!

'You look all-in, Mister Maguire,' said Mary Jo, pulling the blanket closer over her shoulders. 'Been a long day. You travelled far?'

From the brink of hell, he thought, the pain in his ribs beginning to throb. 'Not far, ma'am. South of here.'

She nodded. 'Travellin' alone isn't always easy, is it?' she smiled. 'Miles come and go without much thought for them when you're by yourself, don't you agree?'

'How come your uncle changed his name?' asked Maguire sharply.

The woman frowned. 'I've no idea,' she answered slowly. 'Folk do, don't they? Must be any one of a hundred reasons, I guess. But pa never said, and I never asked.' She fingered the blanket again. 'Does it matter?'

'No, ma'am, maybe not. Like yuh say, folk do.' Especially when they take to killing and robbing, he thought. 'Yuh ever meet him?'

'No, I never did,' said the woman. 'Pa said as how Sam – that was his real name – left home

32

quite young. He was the wild one of the family. Never settled to homesteading.'

You bet he never did, thought Maguire.

'He drifted west, Pa reckoned, and they kinda lost touch. But Pa must've heard somethin' of him, I guess. Somebody must've brought news of him.'

A passing marshal brandishing a Wanted notice, mused Maguire.

'Pa thought a lot of him, I know that. He was just sad Sam never came home again . . . .'

Not surprising, thought Maguire.

'Still, I guess he's out here somewhere. Probably settled down by now.' The woman smiled softly. 'Taken to the quiet life maybe.'

Quiet as roused rattlers in a nosebag! Maguire shifted and held his hands to the fire glow. If he was going to tell her, if he had the guts for it . . . .

'Where you headin' now, Mister Maguire?'

'Oh, here and there, ma'am. Nevada way eventually.'

'Then we'll be partin' company once clear of these hills.'

Maguire stiffened. 'How come, ma'am?'

'Well, you'll be turnin' west. I'm trailin' directly north.'

'North? Why directly north?'

'Oh, it's a long shot, really. Just intuition,' said Mary Jo. 'Probably nothin' in it, but Pa once told as how Uncle Sam – Clant Warre by then,

o' course – always trailed into a place called
Sentiment come high summer. I've no idea why.
Perhaps he has family there, friends maybe, or
could be a home. Anyhow, it's all I've got to go
on, and it is high summer, isn't it?'

'Sure,' gulped Maguire, leaning back from the
glow. 'But Sentiment's one helluva haul from
here, ma'am. Rough country too. No place for a
lone woman.' He felt a line of cold sweat
breaking in his neck. Sentiment, he pondered;
he would never have guessed, not in a dozen
years, that Warre would hole-up there.

'I'll manage,' smiled Mary Jo. 'I'll have to, no
choice. Still . . . . Time to turn in, I reckon.' She
came to her feet and hugged the blanket round
her. 'Thanks again, Mister Maguire – for
everythin'. I'll be sorry when we have to part,
but I wish you well in Nevada. Goodnight.'

Maguire watched in silence as the woman
melted into the shadows. 'Hell!' he mouthed
when she was gone. Now what? How in
tarnation was he going to follow Mary Jo
Goldway to Sentiment without telling her why
he was going there?

'Hell!'

SIX

Maguire had no stomach for sleep that night and was still seated at the fire long after the glow had faded and only wisps of grey smoke curled from the embers.

No stomach for sleep, and no mind for much else – not even the pain in his ribs – save how to face the coming day and deal with Mary Jo Goldway.

They would be clear of the hill range soon after noon, he reckoned. There the trail would fork: to the long plains haul to the west, to the bleak, rocky tracks heading north. The woman would expect him to turn west, and he would have no excuse for not doing so. Not the slightest.

So maybe he would have to turn west then double back to the north on a more remote trail in a few days time. Maybe. Or maybe, between now and noon, he could concoct some story to convince Mary Jo that he had a sudden need to head north. Maybe. Or maybe he would just pray that something turned up – that, or ride out right now.

He had no stomach either for any of the options.

But it could be that the woman was wrong, that Warre had not headed for Sentiment. She had no real proof that he had, only her intuition. Did a man ever set any store by a woman's intuition, he wondered? Sure he did, especially when it was a better prospect than his own vague figuring!

He had nothing to lose.

But Mary Jo sure as hell had plenty to lose once she discovered the truth of 'Uncle Clant's' quiet life! That would be some price to pay for intuition.

Maguire had left the embers of the fire and strolled, still muttering round his options, to the mounts at the hitchline at the far end of the clearing when a sound some way off caught his attention.

He paused, listened, waited for the sound to return. There it was again, distant but closing; the slow, careful movement of a horse under tight rein, a rider in no hurry, watchful and concentrating.

Maguire frowned, turned to be sure the woman was still sleeping, and slid into the darkness of the trees.

The first light was no more than a soft crease in the east, but sufficient even here in the close-hugged pines for him to pick his way with care through the fallen cones and twigs. He went easily, softly in the direction of where he had last heard the sound. Now the early morning was silent and empty, waiting for dawn.

Maybe the rider had halted. Could be he too was waiting. Or watching.

Who was he watching?

Maguire paused a moment and narrowed his gaze on the thinner sprawl of trees ahead. There was probably a track beyond them, he figured. And if there was a rider out here at this hour, that is where he would be. Maguire moved again, almost on tiptoe, bent low, eyes keen as a hawk's.

He had no hankering in his present state of mind for the company of nosy strangers. None at all.

'No fire, Mister Maguire? We all out of fuel or somethin'?' Mary Jo turned from packing her bedroll and stared hard at Maguire. He looked tired, she thought. Maybe he had not slept so well.

'No, ma'am, no fire,' said Maguire. 'Fact is, we're pullin' out right now. Be obliged if yuh'd do what yuh gotta do fast as yuh can.'

The woman frowned and settled her hat on her head with a petulant thrust. 'Why the rush? Heck, it's barely light yet.'

'I know, ma'am. I got eyes.' He swung round from tending his mount and fixed his gaze like a tight shadow on the woman's face. 'Yuh see any other scum with them critters who hit yuh wagon?'

'Others? You mean more men?'

'Just that, ma'am.'

Mary Jo shrugged. 'Can't say. There might have been more. Wasn't takin' a deal of notice once those two were on my tail. Why do you ask?'

'Cus we're bein' trailed. One of 'em's close right now, and there may be more.'

'You've seen them?'

'Seen one an hour back,' said Maguire. 'Must've caught the drift of the smoke from last night's fire.'

The woman came closer. 'Did you speak to him? Didn't you ask him who he was? Maybe he was lost.'

Maguire sighed. 'No, ma'am, I didn't. He didn't look the sociable type, and he sure as hell wasn't lost.'

'How can you be sure?'

'I'm sure, ma'am,' said Maguire, impatiently. 'Now, will yuh saddle up?'

'Where we headin'?'

'North, like yuh said.'

'But shouldn't we wait to meet this man? Perhaps go find him?'

Maguire's gaze darkened. 'Yuh got a lot to learn, ma'am, and the lessons are goin' to come thick and fast!'

They were two miles beyond the clearing and trailing higher into the hill range when the light broke full and white.

The trees had thinned a deal and given way to rough brush, stony slopes and fiercer outcrops of rock from where the shadows lunged like bodies – headless, limbless, and sightless.

Maguire's wary gaze had seen nothing of the rider he had spotted earlier. And there was no sound of him – or was there more than one? Maybe the fellow had waited until full dawn before coming closer to the fire. Maybe he was there now, wondering which way to follow. Or maybe he was a deal smarter and already up ahead.

One thing was for sure, Maguire's first sight of him had left no doubt in his mind that the fellow was from the same mould as the scum he had shot back there at the wagon.

Mary Jo Goldway might not agree; she doubtless would have reckoned the critter a lone rider making his peaceful way, and smelled nothing of him, seen nothing of the mean look in his eyes, the fidgety flick of his hands. Gun hands – and a mite too anxious for comfort.

She might have a lively intuition, but she was bottom of the class in learning the ways of this sort of country and the critters populating it. She had plenty to come to terms with, and the sooner the better.

Maguire reined up and waited for the woman to draw alongside him.

'I'm goin' up ahead a mite,' he said. 'Take the trail horses and hold to this track. No movin' off it. Yuh understand?'

The woman's chin hardened. 'Sure, anythin' you say, Mister Maguire,' she answered, without tempering the note of sarcasm in her voice. 'You're the boss.'

Maguire made no comment save to growl at the mare as he moved away.

Typical, thought Mary Jo, watching him go. Fellow was going to prove a point even if there was no point to be proven. He was out to show her . . . .

And then she froze where she sat at the sound of the fall of a hoof, the creak of leather at her back, and smelled something on the air that had not been there before.

Something very like fear. Her own.

SEVEN

'Let go them trail mounts, lady, and come round real slow.'

The voice grated as if stones were being ground to dust between cold steel. Mary Jo could feel the man's breath, smell the sweat, human and animal, that lathered the air. She shuddered, dropped the rope to the pack horses, and reined her mount round slowly, her eyes suddenly aching and unblinking.

The man's face fitted the voice: a thrown together heap of features that slid like loose grease in a lopsided sprawl from the brow to the chin. The man's stare was icy and consuming, drawing the woman to him, his lips wet in a twitching grin. He shrugged beneath the rag-bag clothing and tightened his grip on his Colt.

'Closer,' he ordered.

Mary Jo urged the mount a step forward. The man holstered his gun, took the reins greedily and chuckled deep in his throat, then swung his gaze through a wide arc to the surrounding trees and the track ahead.

'Where's the fella?' he snapped.

Mary Jo's mouth opened, but no sound came from it.

'Don't matter none,' growled the man, curling the reins to a tighter grip round his wrist. 'Get to him later. You first.' The grin dripped saliva.

'Who – who are you?' stammered Mary Jo. 'What do you want?'

The man grunted through a sideways leer. 'A pay-back, lady – long and sweet as it comes. And yuh're goin' to be the one payin' up for what happened to my friends back there. They're eatin' dust, and we don't take kindly to that.'

'We?' asked Mary Jo.

'Enough talkin'! Let's move!'

The man tugged at the reins, jolting the woman upright in the saddle. Her thoughts scrambled through panic. Where was Maguire? What was he doing? Had he abandoned her? Maybe she should call out. But her voice seemed lost and empty.

She was pulled forward as the man swung his horse towards the treeline. 'Me and Frank are sure goin' to have ourselves one helluva time with you, lady!' he sneered. 'Just one helluva time!'

Mary Jo felt sweat, cold and clinging, across her shoulders, the trickle of it down her back. Perhaps she should throw herself to the ground. But why did she seem clamped to the saddle? Why were her hands so numb and lifeless? Why was the light swinging, turning to a grey shimmering haze? Where had the silence come from? Perhaps she was going to pass out. God willing that she would.

She slumped, rolled, began to slip. The sweat was colder, the light thinner, fading. She could see the man but hear nothing of him. Her eyelids flickered. There was no more light . . . .

But now she was suddenly wide awake.

There was someone – someone moving out of the trees, his hands free of the reins in the levelled hold and aim of a Winchester. His mount came on easy, aware of the rider's intent without a sound or touch of command. A dark figure now with the light at his back; a shadow, alive and covering the ground as if breathed over it; coming on relentlessly without breaking pace.

Mary Jo heard the roar of the shot, saw the flash and glint of the barrel – the cold, impassive look on Maguire's face as he watched his blood-soaked victim crash from his mount in a swirl of limbs and clothes and sprawl like a grotesque outcrop of flesh in the scrub and dirt.

Seconds later, Maguire had grabbed the reins of her mount and was leading her back to the track and the pack horses.

Not a word had passed the tight line of his lips.

They had trailed higher in silence for a half-hour before Maguire was conscious of Mary Jo's fierce glare on his back.

She had recovered from her ordeal at the hands of the scumbag drifter, shaken off the fear, but now she was angry. Oh, yes, thought Maguire, she was angry, like a spooked rattler, and the venom of that anger was fast coming his way!

Maguire heard the click of her tongue as she urged her mount forward to draw alongside him, and then saw the toss of her head, the swirl of hair across her shoulders.

'You left me back there, Maguire,' she flared. 'You hear that? You left me! Heck, I could've been – '

'But you weren't,' snapped Maguire. 'Not even close to it.'

'That isn't the point, damn it! I was scared clean out of my skin, and that's the truth. Another minute and – God knows what might've happened. That fella had only one thing in mind, and I was as close to satisfyin' it as . . . .'   She huffed and tugged at the reins. 'You were lucky, you know that? Dead lucky.'

'Yuh reckon?' said Maguire.

'I reckon. Fella would've gotten clean away with me if he'd held to the track 'stead of headin' for the trees. That was lucky – lucky for you, mister.'

Maguire reined his mount up sharply and stared hard at the woman. 'Or mebbe I figured on him doin' just that.'

'That's easy to say now, mister, but the way I see it — '

'That's the trouble, ma'am,' scowled Maguire, 'yuh don't *see* a deal, and with due respect yuh *know* even less.' He pulled defiantly at the brim of his hat. 'Now I'm tellin' yuh straight – once and once only, so yuh'd best pin back them pretty ears and listen good. Another hour and we'll top these hills and be into clear country to the main trail. That sonofabitch partner of the fella eatin' dirt back there ain't goin' to risk followin' us, not in the open he ain't, but he sure as hell ain't goin' to give up. We've mebbe stirred a whole nest of the varmints, and they're goin' to keep comin' sure as day to night, so we gotta think good and do even better. Yuh got that? Yuh understand?'

Mary Jo tossed her head again. 'What do you have in mind? You goin' to hide or somethin'?

Wait 'til the fellas have passed on? That goin' to be your strategy, Mister Maguire?'

Maguire's stare darkened. 'No, ma'am, nothin' like it. We keep movin', fast as we can; no slowin' down, not for anythin', and if yuh still figurin' on headin' north for Sentiment, then I'm comin' with you – all the way. T'ain't in my nature to desert a woman in danger.'

'Maybe I could —' began Mary Jo.

'Mebbe nothin',' snapped Maguire. 'Intuition ain't goin' to keep them clothes on yuh back. I might – so that's the way of it. Now, let's cut the squawlin' and put some dirt between us and whatever we got sittin' on our butts!'

Another half-hour and Maguire was at peace with the silence. Mary Jo had stopped glaring and was riding easy. The day stood clear and bright, the land ahead was empty, and he already had a sight in the far distance of the main trail to the north.

Things were looking a deal better. Something *had* turned up to keep him within reach of Clant Warre. Two days ride, three at the outside, and they would be in Sentiment. He would make the killing of Warre and his sidekicks a quick affair. No messing. Straight shooting; collect the bounty and head west for Nevada. Only trouble was – the woman. Hell, she would have to take her chance along with the rest.

Who cared, anyhow?

EIGHT

They made good miles through the long, hot day as Maguire held to the main trail where it crossed an open vista from the hill range to the distant roll of the plains.

No chance here, he reckoned, of whoever it was following them making a strike; they would wait for the next cover, maybe save their efforts for the night, or just keep coming on until the mood for an attack took hold. Right now, they were probably licking their wounds and firing up for the kill – save that they would have no plan to end the woman's life. Not for her the quick stab of hot lead. No such luck. Mary Jo's fate would not come so easy.

Even so, Maguire's concentration on the surrounding country stayed tight. Could be they might catch the curl of smoke from a homestead's chimney, or maybe there was a staging post up ahead, assuming Sentiment had ever rated a stage run. Either would do as a break for the woman; a few hours for her to rest up, and a chance to find some breathing space for himself, give his aching limbs some time to simmer down. Hell, he could still feel the thud of Stick Grieves's boot . . . .

But Maguire's luck on that day as it slid to the first shadows of dusk was clean out. No curl of smoke and no hint of a staging post. Nothing save the long drift of the land and the silent emptiness.

'We'll hole-up at the ridge ahead,' he called to the woman. 'Horses need to cool off before nightfall.'

And maybe that goes for you too, ma'am, he mused, with a soft grin!

They drank tepid water and ate jerky. No fire, Maguire had ordered again, as he tended the mounts. And not a deal of talking either, he hoped. Sounds carried on the sultry night.

'We stayin' here 'til sun-up?' asked Mary Jo when Maguire had eased himself into a comfortable drift of sand and rock.

'Two hours at most,' he answered through a weary sigh. 'No more. We move on in the dark. T'ain't the best, but we need the miles.'

'You reckon we're still bein' followed?'

'I do, ma'am, but I'm figurin' on them scumbags needin' to rest up just as much as we do. They're only human – sorta.'

The woman was silent for a moment, scuffing sand under her boot and watching the marks without seeing them. 'Guess I'm glad you came along,' she said at last without lifting her eyes to Maguire. 'I'm grateful. I'd be kinda lost by now if you weren't here. Maybe dead.'

'No, ma'am,' murmured Maguire, 'you wouldn't be dead, but yuh'd sure be wishin' you were.'

The woman's eyes flashed. 'You don't have much of an opinion of folk, do you, Mister Maguire?'

'Only what I see, ma'am – greed-bitten critters for the most part; scumbags, looters, gun-crazed kids and whiskered old robbers. Then there's the rest, but there ain't so many of them. They come up like gold nuggets, but yuh sure as hell have to look real hard.'

'Isn't that very cynical?'

'Not when yuh starin' down a gun barrel it ain't!'

'Well, I hope you don't have any such opinions of me.'

Maguire smiled. 'No, ma'am, I don't. Could kinda get to likin' yuh – for a woman, that is – specially when yuh ain't fumin' so and tempered-up fit to bust.' He settled back and tipped the brim of his hat. 'Time to settle, if yuh ain't goin' to waste yuh couple hours. I'll wake yuh when it's time to saddle. Night, ma'am.'

Mary Jo watched the man for a long minute. She was glad there was no firelight. He might have seen her blushes.

She never knew why she woke so suddenly, or what disturbed her, only that one moment she was in a deep, exhausted sleep, in the next staring wide-eyed into the moon-dappled darkness.

She sat upright, tense and tight, unaware of the cold night chill but alive to every sound that moved through and round it like circling watchers. She looked quickly to where Maguire should have been sleeping in the drift. The space was empty. Her eyes narrowed on the hitch-line. The mounts were still there, quiet and watchful. Things were just as she had seen them before sleep, save for the man. Where in hell was Maguire?

She moved slowly, carefully, turning aside the blanket. Maybe he was keeping watch some place else. Maybe he had heard a sound, gone to investigate. Perhaps the men following them had closed in. But if they had, if they were here now, somewhere in the shadows, why the silence?

She came slowly to her knees, waited, listened. All she could hear was the click of insects, the soft snort of a horse, her own breathing. Times like this she wished she had a gun; wished even more she knew how to use one! But that was one thing Pa had never taught her.

She rummaged through her saddlebags for the knife she always carried, and closed her fingers tight on the handle. She was not too sure she knew how to use that either!

She stood upright and waited again. Still no movements, no sounds. The darkness around her was thick with shapes, contorted and weird, like hanging ghosts filled, it seemed, with eyes that watched without blinking. She shivered now against the chill and moved away towards the deepest shadows.

Supposing she was alone? Supposing Maguire had heard something and discovered that some*thing* had turned out to be some*one*, and there had been no time to defend himself?

Supposing he was dead, out here, somewhere in the night, sprawled in the dirt, a blade in his back?

She was conscious of the sudden weight of the knife in her hand; glanced at it, saw the glint of its sharpness. She had only ever used it to peel a fruit. Hell! Time came when everything had to be put to other uses.

She took another half-dozen steps, peered round her, looked back at the mounts. There had to be someone out here. No one could just disappear, soundless and shapeless, be swallowed by the night and never seen again. No, that did not happen, not for real, so there had to be someone.

There was.

He was there, dangling at the end of a rope lashed round the stricken limb of a dead tree. A long, thin streak of body and clothes, the head lolling, mouth open on the bulge of the blown tongue; turning slowly now in the draught of night air so that the eyes caught at the moonlight and gleamed in a wild, blind stare.

Mary Jo shuddered and felt nothing in her frozen stillness, as if no more than a block of stone, her throat cracked and dry, her eyes stinging. The knife dropped from her fingers. She heard the soft thud as it hit dirt, heard the silence close in again save for the painful creak of the rope round the branch and what seemed through her mind to be the mournful, distant echo of a man throttling to his death.

And then she heard the scuff of a boot into sand at her back.

NINE

She was a long time turning. The seconds seemed to drift through a void of the night, the creaking rope, the sounds of insects, the beat of her heart and the breathing that threatened to choke.

Then she came round slowly as if propelled by her own trembling.

Maguire!

He stood against the darkness like a part of it, not moving, simply watching, his stare as tight and impassive as ever, his eyes incredibly bright, round and white as shining moons.

'What — ' began Mary Jo, and gulped in the effort.

'We had a visitor,' murmured Maguire. 'Came in on foot from some place. Guess he reckoned on sussin' out how things stood. Never made it.'

'You did *that*?' croaked Mary Jo. 'You hanged him?'

'Didn't wanna set up any noise. Might've brought in others, but I figure now he was the last of the bunch. Reckon we're in the clear from here on.' Maguire's stare flicked to the dead body. 'Sonofabitch went out fittin'.'

Mary Jo gulped again, shivered against the chill of cold sweat, but gazed with an unblinking look of incredulity filling her eyes.

'How could you do that?' she croaked. 'How could you? A perfect stranger, someone you'd never seen before, never said a word to. You just hanged him – in cold blood.'

'Not a deal of choice, ma'am,' shrugged Maguire. 'Him or me. Odds were even.'

'But he could have been anyone – anyone, a drifter, somebody just passin' through, maybe in need of help.' Mary Jo shivered again. 'He was a human bein', for God's sake. You couldn't possibly have known – '

'He weren't here for no coffee, ma'am. He was here to kill me.'

'You don't know that,' said the woman, beginning to flare as a flush of anger came to her cheeks. 'I don't suppose you *asked* him!'

'No, ma'am, I didn't. No need. I gotta kind of instinct for knowin' when a fella's set on killin' me! It comes as second nature.'

'And your first is killin', Mister Maguire. Cold-blooded killin'!' Mary Jo's voice rose a pitch. 'In God's name, what are you? What do you think, what do you feel? Nothin'. You can't possibly feel anythin'. Ever!' A shudder passed through her like the touch of a cold hand. 'In a matter of a few hours you've killed four men, mister. Four men! And this one you hanged. Does the killin' ever stop for you? Does it? Do you enjoy it? Have you always enjoyed it? How many men have you killed, f'Crissake?'

Maguire settled his hands on his hips. 'I ain't been keepin' a count, ma'am!' he sighed. 'But if I put my mind to it and get to thinkin' back — '

Mary Jo kicked furiously at the sand. 'I don't want to hear! I don't want to know. I don't want to go on lookin' at you, mister. I want to get you clean out of my life – for good, fast as I can. Right now!'

'Suit y'self, ma'am. It's your life. Just be grateful yuh still got one.'

'Grateful! Grateful? Oh, yes, I'm grateful, Maguire, that I surely am, and now the gratitude is over. Finished. Do you hear? Finished. I'm ridin' out. I'm goin', and you can carry on with your killin' wherever and whenever you want. I'm not goin' to be around to see it, or hear it, or smell it. And I sure as hell ain't goin' to have you in my sights.' Mary Jo tossed her hair defiantly into her shoulders. 'And may God

57

have some mercy on you when you're facin' Hell!'

'Amen,' groaned Maguire, and watched the woman disappear like a tornado into the night.

Morning came up high and full and warm on the twist of smoke from Maguire's fire. He watched the lick of thin flame and reckoned it might be some time before he tasted hot coffee again. The woman had left him with just enough for a single brew, and ridden out – with the packhorses!

He grunted and ran a hand over his already sticky face. He could do with a wash, a decent meal, some sleep, but all three looked remote; no nearby stream, no food, and no time for resting up, not if he was going to be in Sentiment and get to Clant Warre ahead of Mary Jo Goldway.

Darn the woman, he thought, still watching the flames. What sort of a fool thing was it to go riding out like that? She sure had led some hell of a sheltered life back there at Willadon. Had she never crossed the paths of the vermin that drifted through the land? Had her Pa been that protective? Or maybe he had seen too much of the scum; suspected his own brother of going the same way. If that had been his thinking, then why send his own daughter into the arms of the man?

Maybe madness ran in the family!

Maguire grunted again. Whatever, Mary Jo had sure had a rude introduction to the darker side of life the day fate threw them together at the shattered wagon. Fact was, though, that the darkness would have closed in real permanent for her had he not been around. She did not see it that way, and maybe he could not blame her.

Maybe he should have told her straight out that survival was the way of things for him if he was ever going to raise enough bounty for that spread in Nevada. Killing, when it came to it, was a throw of equal odds – and he had a natural-born winning hand, leastways a faster draw.

He shrugged. Maybe too he should have told her about Clant Warre and his sidekicks. She might have seen things different; might have done the sensible thing and headed straight back to Willadon. She would do that anyhow once she faced the grim truth at Sentiment. *If* she made it to Sentiment, and *if* she made it out of the place.

Meantime, he pondered, scratching his neck, she was out there alone in wild country. Well, she would just have to learn the hard way. She had made the choice; she would have to stand to it. No point in getting weak-minded about what might happen. She would find out soon enough, and there were other matters to get to if he was going to make it to Nevada before the Fall.

Mary Jo Goldway did not figure in any of them.

'Yuh two-bits liar!' he murmured to himself as he scuffed sand into the fire. Who was he kidding? He could no more turn his back on that darned woman than he could shoot his mount. Hell, he knew well enough he was going to trail her fast as he could, catch up with her, and no matter how hard she spat her disgust see her safe to Sentiment.

What happened after that . . . .

That would have to wait. No man could handle more than his fair share, especially when a fire-tempered woman was prancing like a frisky heifer on the other end of the rope!

'Damnit!' he grunted, dousing the fire. 'Damn-damn-damnit!'

Ten minutes later he had packed, saddled up and turned the mare's head to the trail north. He looked back with the merest glance at the man hanging from the tree. Scumbag would have shown Mary Jo no mercy, you could bet on that, he mused. But he sure as hell would have raised her disgust to boiling point.

Guess the little minx had never figured that.

*　*　*

Nor, when it came to noon and the sun stood high and the heat seared the land like flame, had Maguire figured on there being so little of the woman's tracks to follow.

He had picked up her trail easily enough at the start as she headed directly north, but why, he wondered, had it begun to peter out within a few miles? And why had it finally faded completely?

Mary Jo had left the main trail and headed – where? East, west? Turned south again? What had prompted her, attracted her?

Or worse, forced her?

TEN

Mary Jo reined back her mount in the lull of the narrow creek and mopped her brow. Not far now, she reckoned. Not if she had been right in the first place.

She had seen the twist of smoke soon after taking to the trail; no more than a whisper of pale grey on the blue sky; there, and then suddenly gone as if the remains of an overnight fire had taken a last breath. Or had it been a mirage, some twist of her imagination, her confused thoughts? Maybe she had been seeing things, but if the smoke had been real she could sure use the comforts of a homestead for a while, not to say the everyday sanity of ordinary folk.

She tied the sweatband at her neck and relished for a moment the cool of the creek shade. It was good to feel free again, to *be* free . . . .

OK, she admitted, so maybe she had lost her temper with Maguire back there, but not her sense of right from wrong. It was wrong to go killing folk, always had been, always would be, more so when the victim had never had a chance to explain himself.

So maybe the two who had hijacked her wagon had been no-gooders, just like the fellow who had tried to take her from the trail – and sure, she was grateful to Maguire, glad he had been around. But the man he had hanged . . . .

Who had he been? Had he deserved to die like that?

Truth of it was, she reckoned, Maguire was a killer, an out-and-out professional who made a dark living that way and who had probably killed so many men he had forgotten a person's right to life. Killing was instinctive, like lifting a finger; a part of him, coursing through his blood like adrenalin, and now he enjoyed it.

Well, let him. She did not have to share it. She did not have to be there to see it. She could not. It sickened her to the gut.

Even so, she frowned, he was good at it; what the men at Willadon would have called a 'fast gun'. And maybe he had been a decent type way back. There must have been a time when his calculating stare had settled with a warmer glow.

Or maybe he had been born that way.

Trouble was, men changed, and for no good reason saving their own pride. She frowned again. Uncle Sam had found a reason to change to the man known now as Clant Warre.

She wondered why, and then smiled softly to herself. She guessed she would have to get used to calling him 'Uncle Clant' once she hit Sentiment.

Mary Jo had trailed eastwards from the creek for another half-hour before she knew for certain that the twist of grey smoke had been no illusion.

There it was, large as life, a chimney atop a roof that sheltered the four stone-built walls of what had once, she thought, been a trading post. Place looked a deal worn and weary now – maybe it had lost the main trail business with the coming of the railroad farther south – but it was civilization, the first she had seen in a long time.

More important, somebody lived there. Horses were hitched in the shade to the right, and the door stood open against the noon heat. And surely that was a brimming water-butt beside the lone, stunted tree. A chance at last of a real wash!

She came slowly over the rocky slope to the post, the packhorses trailing easy behind her, her gaze tight on the open door and the welcome it promised. Maybe someone would catch a sight of her, though she guessed there were not too many visitors to such a remote place. Chances were the folk would be glad of the sight of a new face, a new voice anxious with the news from other parts.

She would get to telling all she knew soon enough, but not before she had relished the pleasures of that water-butt and changed out of her dusty clothes. She might even wear a dress come sundown. The blue one Pa had always liked so much . . . .

The man grew in the shadow of the doorway like a smear of light and stood there, leaning on the jamb, smoking a cheroot, for a full minute before throwing the smoke to the sand and disappearing indoors again.

Mary Jo had waved, but maybe the man had not seen her against the glare of the sun. Or perhaps he had gone to call his wife, maybe the whole family. Imagine that – real kids! Must be some surprise to them to see a woman riding in trailing two packhorses. Not an everyday occurrence.

She moved on steadily. Heck, she thought, there was no rush, not when you were this close to a welcoming spread. Pity she and Maguire had not found the place the night before. Might have made a whole lot of difference to everything – and spared a man his vile end.

She wondered with a sudden start if Maguire had seen the same brief twist of smoke. Maybe not. Chances were he had headed west for Nevada, glad to have shed his troublesome company and free now to go on shooting and hanging his way clear through to wherever he planned to settle his butt next.

She cleared the rocky slope and came to the soft sand fronting the post. She could distinguish the faint remains of the trail that had once passed this way heading east. That must have been years back, she thought. Strange that folk had chosen to stay on miles from anywhere, with only sand and rock for neighbours. Still, you might raise horses here, given a constant supply of fresh water.

No horses, save the hitched and saddled mounts, she noted. No corral. And no stream.

She had come to within a few yards of the post and reined up when the man who had watched her trailing in reappeared in the doorway and resumed his lazy stance at the jamb.

'Mornin' – I mean afternoon . . . howdy,' smiled Mary Jo, relaxing the reins. 'Sure is a warm one, specially out there on the trail. Saw your smoke and figured I might rest up awhile. Hope you don't mind. Guess you don't get to seein' too many visitors.'

The man stayed silent, relaxed, simply watching, the gaze from the slant of his grey eyes moving over her like the probe of a shaft of light.

Mary Jo's smile flickered again, this time nervously. 'Mind if I step down?' she asked.

'Sure, help y'self,' said the man, standing straight. 'Yuh welcome. More than welcome.'

Mary Jo slid to the sand and dusted her clothes. 'Know somethin', I'd give a whole lot for a chance to wash-up and change. Trail dirt eats right into you.'

The man's fingers twitched like eager tendrils at his sides. 'Yeah,' he drawled, 'I guess it does at that. Right through yuh. All over.'

Mary Jo stiffened and stood perfectly still, a cooler tingle moving over her spine, and felt a nerve jump in her arm as a second man grew in the shadow of the doorway.

'Well, now, look yuh here, will yuh?' he grinned. 'A real woman, I do declare! Ain't she a sight, eh, Loose? Ain't she just.'

'Sure is, Stick,' murmured his partner. 'One helluva sight.'

And for the first time that hot, airless day Mary Jo shivered.

ELEVEN

Say one thing for the darned fool woman, thought Maguire, taking a long draught from his canteen, she sure made haste.

He wiped the back of his hand across his mouth, spat into the sand, then narrowed his gaze on the high sky. He had three, maybe four hours before dusk began to settle; time enough to keep tracking the woman, if only he knew which way to go, damnit!

He led the mare deeper into the shade of the boulders and shaded his eyes in a scan of the land around him. Not a deal to go on, he mused, and nothing of a hint as to the trail the woman had taken. So what *might* she have done?

She had left the main trail north, that was for certain. She had not doubled back to the south,

which left west and the east. The land sprawl
eastwards rose and fell through a series of
hidden creeks and gulches to a distant range of
hills. The spread westwards petered out from
rock to empty plain, and beyond that maybe
little more than desert. Nothing there, he
thought, for someone who could read the
terrain. But that was it – Mary Jo could not read
it! She would trust to luck, or whatever took her
fancy. Or maybe that old-fashioned intuition.

Or was there another factor to reckon on?

It could be, he figured, that she might just
have a hankering for more homely comforts:
roof over her head, table to sit at, bed to sleep in,
somewhere to take a long bath. That would be
woman's thinking as he recalled it, and maybe
more so in Mary Jo's case, taking into account
her frame of mind. Yep, he pondered, you could
bet on it . . . somewhere to rest up for a night or
so, clear her head and get to thinking straight
again; dust herself down from the dirt of death.

Maguire grunted and fixed his gaze on the
east.

If there was any place where a man might
have settled, it would be out there among the
creeks where the land rose and fell, where there
would be natural shelter and the best chance of
water.

Mary Jo might not have figured it quite like
that, but she might have *seen* something.

A twist of smoke?

Maguire grunted again and stiffened. Sky was clear enough now. Not a cloud, nothing save the endless blue. But there could have been something – that twist of smoke maybe – hours back.

Seemed like he had no choice. On the other hand, there was Sentiment and the chance of Clant Warre. Well, maybe Warre would have to wait awhile.

He went back to the mare; mounted up and reined her head to the east. 'Darned fool woman!' he murmured. 'Go gettin' herself in real trouble if she ain't careful.'

Mary Jo watched the shadows and the hot, sweating faces filling them: the two men who had greeted her at the post, men who were saying little now, who simply stood there, watching her, as if consumed by a maze of thoughts, wondering which to follow, and when.

A third man, a half-breed, part Apache, she reckoned, who had said nothing so far, done nothing save to serve the other two with cheap, musty whiskey, also watched and waited.

The room at the post was heavy with the smell of drink, mingling with the stench of long-ago cooking, sweat, dust and dirt. She could make out ageing boxes, barrels, fading cloths and blankets, the forgotten flotsam of a once thriving store.

The half-breed stood behind a stained bar, the faint, flickering glow of a lantern at his elbow. The two men leaned on the wall opposite where the shadows were deepest; mean, hungry shadows that had been there since the place was built and had no intention of leaving.

Mary Jo swallowed on a throat that seemed caked with dust. 'I'm makin' for Sentiment,' she said in a stumbling clutter of words. 'Had a wagon when I began, but that. . . . Well, don't matter none now, I suppose. I saw your smoke back there on the trail. Thought I might . . . . You fellas headin' for Sentiment by any chance?'

She felt her fingers begin to twist together in a heap in her lap, a trickle of sweat slide from her neck to her breasts where it lay like melting ice. Her eyes ached, her heart thudded. She was beginning to feel numb under the men's relentless stares, pinned down by them. She glanced quickly at the half-open door. Maybe she should leave, right now, before —

'Could I have a glass of water, please?' she heard herself croak.

The half-breed waited for a nod from the older man before slopping water into a tin mug and bringing it to her. She drank eagerly, anxiously, hoping that the liquid might last forever.

Or that she might float away in it.

'Is it far?' she began again. 'To Sentiment, I mean? I've never been this far west, or is it north? I'm not very good at these things. No sense of direction! Never did have . . . . Not even as a kid. Not that I'm in any great hurry. Well, I suppose I am really. Wouldn't want to be too long out here, what with the heat and everything . . . .'

The words faded. The stares closed in. The younger man mopped the sweat from his neck. His partner licked his lips .

'What sort of a place is Sentiment, anyhow?' Mary Jo tried to smile, but the effort collapsed in a tremble of lips. 'Very big? Or just a small place? Small, I guess. An outpost town kinda. I have a relation there. Maybe you know him. Folk know most everybody in a small town, don't they? We did back at Willadon. Just about everybody knew everybody, and if a stranger rode in . . . that was somethin'. But I guess my relation ain't exactly no stranger to the town. I would reckon . . . . '

The younger man sighed noisily. 'Well, mebbe we'll get to showin' yuh, lady. Mebbe. All in good time. In a day or so, eh, Loose? When we're all through. Right now we're kinda restin' up awhiles; takin' it easy.' His grin spread like a slow stain. 'Meantime, glad of yuh company. Ain't that so, Loose? Real glad.'

'Sure,' said the older man. He turned to the

half-breed. 'Yuh got somethin' better to do? Well, do it! Now. And close the door behind yuh.'

Mary Jo saw the shadows move, heard them in the steps that came closer. Saw too the eyes that devoured her in their gleam and did not blink.

It was evening in a blaze of sunset that threw the light like scattered jewels when Maguire reached the narrow creek where Mary Jo had paused earlier that day.

No doubt about it, he thought, holding the mare head-on to the freshening breeze, the woman had been here, passed this way and continued directly east. The tracks were clear enough. So what had she seen?

It had to be a twist of smoke, he reckoned. There was no other explanation. But not the smoke from a settled homestead. No, this country was too remote and barren for that. An old trail trading post? Some place that was still home to whoever had decided to stay on after the railroad boom? That figured. Not exactly teeming with homely comforts, but it would be a roof and maybe a bed.

Leastways, that would have been Mary Jo's fond hope.

The night was gathering fast in long, deep

shadows by the time Maguire had his first glimpse of the post. It was occupied, sure enough; soft glow of a single lantern at the window meant that somebody was home. Only trouble was . . . .

Maguire had sat for some time watching the place like a hawk at its spotted prey before being convinced that he was right; if Mary Jo had been here – and he reckoned that was for certain – she had since saddled up and moved on again. There was only one mount hitched, a good-looking palomino.

Maguire grunted quietly, tightened his grip on the reins and urged the mare to a soft saunter to the post. There was no hurry, no need to announce his arrival too soon to whoever looked beyond that lantern glow. They could watch if they wanted, but they had sure as hell best not move too fast through that door. He might just get jumpy.

And the glint of light on the Winchester's barrel might be the last they would see before a very permanent night closed in.

TWELVE

Maguire had halted the mare just short of the front of the building when he caught the softest drift of a shadow at the window.

Somebody had been watching; somebody who had moved now to the door, maybe had a hand on the latch, was waiting for a sound, a voice, the courage to will his hand to move again.

'Do it now, mister,' murmured Maguire to himself, his eyes narrowed, fingers tense on the rifle. 'What yuh waitin' for?'

The door opened slowly on a creak of sad hinges; at first no more than a chink through which a shaft of light scuttled like something released, then wider until the shaft thickened and grew. The mare pawed nervously at sand. Maguire's grip tightened on the reins. Another creak, more light. A pause. Silence.

'Don't shoot.'

The words from behind the door lay on the night as if hung there.

Maguire grunted and backed the mare. The door swung open and the half-breed stood in the space, legs apart, arms stiff at his sides, the whites of his eyes as bright as moons.

'Yuh alone here?' asked Maguire. The half-breed nodded. 'Been a woman through today?'

A nerve twitched in the 'breed's cheek, his fingers flexed. 'Sometime back. They took her.'

His eyes flicked to the dark spread of the hills.

'They?' frowned Maguire. 'Who's they?'

'Two men. Stick Grieves and Loose Carne.'

The sweat broke like a burst vessel in Maguire's neck and his grip on the Winchester was suddenly numb. 'Yuh sure?' he croaked. The 'breed nodded again. 'Fella by the name of Warre been here?'

The 'breed shrugged. 'Just two,' he murmured. 'Grieves and Carne.'

'What about the woman? She OK ?'

The 'breed's eyes darkened as he stood aside from the doorway. 'See,' was all he said as Maguire slid from his mount, slipped the Winchester to its scabbard and moved into the post.

He blinked in the sullen glow of the lantern light and sniffed on the lingering smells of dirt, old dust, sweat and liquor. Tin mugs and glasses littered the bar, an empty bottle lay at the foot of it. One hell of a hole, he thought, moving deeper into the room. Sure would have shattered Mary Jo's hopes.

And then he stiffened.

The torn remnants of the woman's clothes were strewn against the far wall, limp, lifeless and stained, a skulking pile in a darkened corner; her shirt, boots, pants, the scarf she had worn at her neck.

Maguire swallowed on a throat that felt as if it had been dragged for a week through parched sand. His mind reeled with images of the woman: the sight of her at the shattered wagon, her riding alongside him, the flare of her temper, the look of disgust in her eyes, the dance of her hair, the sigh when she had talked of what she might find at a town called Sentiment.

'What in hell happened here?' he grunted as the half-breed joined him.

'What you see is what happened,' said the 'breed. 'And will happen again – until the woman is dead.'

The clear night air cleared the stench from Maguire's nostrils; the starlit space outside the frost settled the images he had seen inside. Now there was only the deep inner anger to lift the prickle of sweat in his neck.

He kicked at a loose stone in the sand and turned to face the 'breed. 'Yuh saw all this?' he asked.

'Heard,' said the man.

'And did nothin'!' snapped Maguire.

The half-breed turned aside the tunic at his neck to show the raw gashes of a pistol whipping. 'They were gone when I moved again.'

Maguire grunted and kicked at another stone. 'Yuh live here? This your place? How come these scum were here, anyhow? They friends of yours or somethin'?' He swallowed on the anger welling in his guts.

'I stayed when the post closed down,' said the 'breed. 'No choice for my kind. Better here than in the town.' He folded his arms across his chest. 'I know these men, it is true. They have been before. Always in the summer. Always from the town. They ride out here to talk, drink. Sometimes just the two. Sometimes three. Then they go.'

'So where 've they taken the woman?'

The 'breed swung his gaze to the hills. 'That way. North-east. They will stay one, two days, until there is nothing to stay for.'

Maguire sighed. 'They gotta helluva head start.' His fingers danced over the butt of his Colt. 'I gotta move. Right now.'

'You follow these men?'

'Yuh bet I follow! Sittin' like a rattler on their scum tails!'

'Hungry rattler go only where food is certain.'

'Meanin'?' frowned Maguire.

'Hills are long and wide. Many trails. Many places to hide. Which trail you choose? Or does hunger blind you?'

'Yuh know these hills?' said Maguire slowly. 'Yuh know them that well? Mebbe yuh know where them sonsofbitches will hole-up? That it?'

The 'breed relaxed his arms. 'Hills are my country.'

'Then show me.'

'You know these men from another place. I see that. I know them. I too am hungry.'

They left the dreary solitude of the post long before the night had cleared, and headed over open country for the sprawl of the hills. The half-breed led, seated easy and relaxed on the palomino, with Maguire trailing silently in his tracks, his thoughts in a turmoil of doubt, disbelief, uncertainty and gut-rooted anger.

Fate had sure dealt a bewildering hand. What price had been the odds, he wondered, of Mary Jo stumbling across Grieves and Carne? Had she had the time or the inclination to mention her 'uncle'? Would she still have the time, and what difference would it make, anyhow, save maybe to scare Warre's sidekicks into getting rid of her sooner than they planned?

They would hardly want to bring 'Uncle Clant's' niece into Sentiment in her state!

Hell, he groaned inwardly, the woman was jinxed; trouble trailed right alongside of her like a long shadow. But whatever her troubles now, they were a lean helping to what lay ahead. If the half-breed failed to pick up the trail, if he did not read the hills as he reckoned he could, if they were so much as only an hour late in finding Grieves and Carne, then Mary Jo's chances of seeing noon were about as remote as horses flying.

Goddamnit, he rued the day he had heard the creaking dash of that wagon and chosen to interfere. Things would have been a whole lot easier for Mary Jo if she had simply turned tail and headed back to Willadon; back to the prim, quiet life where she belonged. And it would have been a darned sight more peaceful for himself. Gunning down Clant Warre would have seemed as gentle as a Sunday morning stroll!

But in the meantime . . . .

His grip on the reins tightened as the half-breed indicated to trail more to the right. Maybe the fellow really was that hungry to catch up with Warre's scumbags.

God willing, it was a hunger that would gnaw on!

THIRTEEN

Mary Jo shuddered at the touch of the damp dawn mist and pulled nervously at the blanket draped across her shoulders. She watched her breath curl into the grey light that hugged the hills, slid like old fingers through the scattering of pines and brush, and blinked her aching, bloodshot eyes on the two men seated in the dip of the clearing.

Animals, they were just mindless animals. 'Bastards!' she mouthed, and felt her bruised lips tremble with the effort. She swallowed on the taste of caked blood and vowed once again that she would not give in – not now, not ever, not until they finally had to shoot her.

And they would, they surely would, because they had no other way out. They had trapped themselves in their filth and drunken lust and realized too late, far too late, that she was who she said she was. Only in that moment, deep into the night when they had taken her between them yet again and she had screamed the name 'Clant Warre' had she seen a look of fear cloud their leering gaze. Only then had they backed off as if brushed by the sudden chill of a haunting they felt was close and knew was real.

That had been the moment when they too had sweated fear, and were still sweating in the morning's cold, clinging air . . . .

'Yuh believe her?' hissed Stick Grieves. 'She tellin' the truth? Yuh figure that's so?'

Loose Carne stared at the dirt at his feet. 'Ain't no other way of explainin' it,' he croaked. 'How else would she know about Clant, about him changin' his name way back? She's gotta be family like she says. Ain't no others savin' us who know Clant's real identity.' He spat. 'She's his niece, sure enough. And that leaves us in one helluva hole.'

Grieves reached for a stray twig, grabbed it and snapped it between his bony fingers. 'We weren't to know. We couldn't have known. Hell, she's a woman, ain't she? Some woman at that – but, goddamn it, I ain't in the habit of askin' for a family history before I help m'self! I see 'em, I take 'em. Simple as that. Same goes for y'self, and yuh can't say other.'

'Ceptin' this time we was plumb wrong, and

Clant ain't goin' to take what we done with no understandin' smile on his face, is he? He ain't goin' to stand there and say "Bad luck, fellas, but no harm done; like yuh say, she's a woman, and a woman's a woman come what may." No, he sure as night ain't goin' to say that! I'll tell yuh just what he's goin' to do . . . I can spell it out like it was as clear as the nose on yuh darned face. Wanna hear? Well, I'll tell yuh, anyhow. . . .'

'No reason for him to know,' said Grieves slowly, his eyes narrowing. 'None at all. Not if he never gets to seein' her. If she ain't around.' His cold gaze flicked to Carne's face. 'Figure it for y'self. We said as how we'd be back in Sentiment in a week. Ain't that so? Right . . . right, and so we shall, just like we said, you and me. Clant ain't goin' to get to hearin' where we been or what we been doin', is he? No way. And even if he does, all he'll hear is that we took ourselves a woman. So? Clant'll be doin' that himself back in town, won't he? He ain't goin' to be one mite interested in *which* woman we had, is he? Why should he? Ain't he always said as how one woman ain't no different from the next? Yuh heard him say that. Yuh heard it times.'

Carne grunted. 'Why was she travellin' alone? How come a woman like that ain't accompanied? Or mebbe she was. And if she was, mebbe she still *is*. Yuh thought of that? Mebbe there's someone out there right now who's closin' in on us, comin' for her. Knowin' full well where she is and, hell, *who* she is!'

'Goddamnit, Loose, yuh sure go spookin' up trouble for y'self, don't yuh! Seein' it when it ain't even breathin' yet! Who the hell cares who the woman might have been with, might not have been with? It don't matter, not a snitch. Ain't nobody savin' that dumb-headed 'breed back at the post who seen us with the woman, and he ain't goin' to come trailin' up here to find her, is he? No chance. He'll just sit there on his butt like he always does and do nothin'. So where's the problem in hell's name?'

'Yeah, well . . . but supposin' . . .' began Carne.

'Supposin' nothin'!' snapped Grieves. 'There ain't no other way: we get rid of the bitch, and that's the end of it. Or ain't yuh got the stomach for killin' a woman?'

Carne's gaze lifted slowly to Grieves's face. 'We could be doin' the wrong thing,' he murmured. ''Bout as wrong as it ever gets.'

'Sure,' drawled Grieves. 'Well, you just get to ponderin' on that while I go settle the issue. F'Crissake, Loose, for a sonofabitch always so hot-pantin' for a woman, yuh sure get to worryin' like one!'

*   *   *

Maguire blinked on a sudden flood of tiredness, stiffened in the saddle and brought his focus back to the curtain of grey dawn mist, the dark shapes of the pines, the hunchback outcrops of rock and, up ahead of him, the half-breed.

They had moved steadily, silently, without pausing through the last of the sand flats to the gentle lift of the foothills to begin the long climb into the high country. The track they had followed had at first been clear and broad enough for a mount to follow almost without the need to rein to it. Easy, Maguire had thought. Anybody could have found it.

But once it had turned, twisted and petered to no more than a hairline through the scratchings of tufts and loose stones, he had thought again. Not so easy, not unless you knew where to find it, or could sense that others had, and not so long back at that. So he had settled his concentration on the 'breed and gone back to wondering if the woman was still alive.

She had guts, he could say that for her; misguided and misplaced, but guts. And that darned fool intuition that had probably led her into this mess in the first place. But there was another side of the problem he was sure not ignoring: he was getting closer a whole lot sooner than expected to at least two of the scum who had beaten him near to death. That was some real consolation, a satisfaction he was going to relish – but, darn it, no comfort to the woman, dead or alive.

He blinked again as the half-breed brought the palomino to a halt and sat without moving, his gaze set like some strange shaft of light on the misty gloom ahead. Maguire waited, tense, his tiredness drifting from him as if taken on some sudden breeze.

He tightened his gaze against the sting of damp air, flexed his fingers into new life on the reins, held his breath, and listened.

Was that a movement, a footfall, somebody coming this way? Real or imagined?

And then it was sharply, violently real in the moan and shuddering scream of the woman.

'Leave it,' said Maguire, coming alongside the half-breed. 'This is my show. All mine.'

He slid from his mount and went like some dark ghost to a haunting in the mist-licked trees. And the half-breed could smell the hatred.

FOURTEEN

There was the look of a killing in his icy gaze; a leer at his lips of the pleasure to come, and a play at his fingers that warned he was keen to get on with it, see it done and be clear of the place.

Mary Jo was sure then that there were only minutes left to her.

She shuddered again as Grieves approached, fingered the blanket and came slowly to her feet. She had no hope of running, no one to call to. Her thoughts swayed through a blur of images: Pa and the homestead, her promise to find her uncle, the wagon, these men – who were they, why had they turned so grey at the mention of Clant Warre? – and Maguire.

What had happened to Maguire? Where was he now? Why had she ridden off like that? Had she been fair – to him, to herself?

And what now – why did Grieves hesitate? Why not shoot her where she stood? Was there anything to be gained, any point in waiting? Do it, for God's sake!

Her low moan grew to a strangled scream, but her fear served only to spread the man's leer to a sickly grin. He paused, eased his weight to one leg, and slid his thumbs into his belt.

'Know somethin', lady,' he drawled, 'I sure am goin' to feel a whole lotta remorse at doin' this. It's a real shame, yuh bein' as good-lookin' as yuh are. And yuh been real nice to me and Loose. Real nice. Pity it's gotta end like this. T'ain't goin' to be one of my better days, and that's for sure.'

Grieves moved forward again; slow, careful steps, his eyes brighter now in the lure of the kill. Mary Jo backed, stumbled, reached into empty space. The blanket began to slip from her shoulders. Her hair lay plastered in her neck. Her lips trembled.

She might in that moment have summoned the strength to run, turn her back on the man and shut out the gleam of the killing in his gaze.

She might – but the sudden crack of a branch in the deeper brush to her right froze her to the spot.

Grieves stopped, stiffened, swung his gaze to the sound, narrowed his eyes and slid a tight, anxious hand to the butt of his Colt. He frowned, waiting for another movement, perhaps a shape, a voice. Maybe Loose had stirred himself to be in at the death. Maybe he wanted just one last look at the woman.

Sure, that would be it. One last look . . . .

And then the morning, its clinging mist and the lame half light were ripped apart in the blaze of a shot that buried lead deep into Stick Grieves's thigh.

He fell with a piping yelp, blood bubbling from the wound. His face twisted into agonized creases under the pain. He began to sweat and stared like some petrified animal into the dark sprawl of brush.

Mary Jo gasped and shuddered, the trees, the ground, brush swirling before her as if tossed to a whirlwind, and gasped again as her eyes widened on the man who stepped from the mist and levelled his still smoking gun at Stick Grieves's head.

'Remember?' murmured Maguire. 'Back there in the desert, the man yuh left for dead? He's back! Right here, Stick. Or mebbe he's just a ghost, eh? Yuh ain't never goin' to know, are yuh? Never really know. . . .'

The second roar of the Colt blew a part of Stick Grieves's face clean away to leave only one of his eyes staring into a sky that was not yet there, and now would never be.

And Mary Jo passed out.

The mist had cleared and the day steamed to already high heat by the time Maguire was satisfied that Mary Jo would be well enough to move come noon.

That, he thought, would be the easy part. A whole lot more of a headache would be figuring just where that move might take her.

Would she turn right around and head back to Willadon, forget the fool business of going on to Sentiment and reckon herself lucky to have survived this far? She would if she had any sense, thought Maguire.

But sense in that regard did not always figure too highly in Mary Jo's reckoning! No, damn it, she was just plumb stubborn enough to keep going due north with Sentiment and her 'uncle' her only concern. And if that were the case . . . .

Maguire stirred the embers of the fire, and cursed. He would have no choice but to tell her the truth about Clant Warre, every darned miserable shred of the sorry story, missing nothing, not a single detail. God knows how she would take it, but she had to be told, and a whole lot more alongside it.

He grunted. She was not going to take kindly either to hearing of his own plans for Warre, not even after what had happened, and that could stir a whole nest of hornets.

So be it; let them be stirred. Facts were facts and no hiding from them no matter which way you turned. Temper and tantrum at their worst, life just happened to be life out here – and tough with it.

Or maybe he should leave the woman here with the half-breed, pick up Carne's trail before he got too far ahead. And that was another thing . . . .

'North,' said the half-breed, coming to the fire. 'Riding fast. He will be in Sentiment in two moons.'

'And get to Warre,' grunted Maguire.

'Who will wait for you if Carne is certain you are the one left for dead. If he saw you.'

'Reckon he did?' asked Maguire.

The half-breed shrugged. 'Perhaps. Saw and ran.'

'I figure so. Suits me.'

'But there is the woman. What do you do with her? Will she believe your story?'

'Do you?' asked Maguire.

'I know these men. I believe you. I believe what you will do.' The half-breed's gaze tightened. 'I have seen who you are. That is enough.'

They turned as Mary Jo stirred behind them. 'And so have I,' she murmured.

FIFTEEN

'You're a bounty hunter, Mister Maguire! A two-bits gunslinger who kills for the price on a man's head and ain't fussed none how high or low the price. And maybe you ain't fussed none either about who you're killin'. Maybe that's why it comes so easy, any place, any time – any man!'

Beat her, abuse her, rape her, it hardly seemed to matter a damn to Mary Jo Goldway. She just came up bubbling and boiling as if nothing had happened, and it sure as hell rankled a man's nerve!

Did nothing soften her, wondered Maguire, watching as she hitched the pants and buttoned the shirt he had taken from the packhorse abandoned by Carne? Hell, she hissed like a stick-stirred rattler!

'But don't go thinkin' I ain't grateful to you for steppin' in like you did,' she flounced on, flicking her hair over her shoulders. 'I am. Mighty grateful. You saved my life – again. And I ain't takin' nothin' of that from you.'

'Well, I'm real obliged to yuh, ma'am!' grunted Maguire through a deep sigh.

Mary Jo shot him a quick, fiery glance. 'Don't change nothin', though,' she continued. 'I'm goin' on to Sentiment. And you want to know why? I'll tell you. I'm goin' to seek out the sheriff there and have that other sonofabitch brought to book for what he did to me. And frankly, Mister Maguire, I'm goin' to enjoy watchin' him hang. I'm goin' to relish every moment, and I might just get to whoopin' when he's strung up there like a side of rotten beef!'

Maguire sighed again and half-closed his eyes.

'That's what I'm goin' to do. As for yourself, well, I suppose you're goin' to load up that stinkin' body there and go claim your prize. That's your business, and you're welcome to it. But just don't go assumin' I'll be ridin' alongside of you while you do it, 'cus I won't. It ain't in my nature to associate myself with such trade, but I'll sure put in a good word for your decency to me when I reach Sentiment. So I'd be obliged if the gentleman there — ' She nodded to the half-breed – 'would escort me the rest of the way. I'll pay, of course.'

'Miss Goldway,' said Maguire carefully, 'before yuh go hustlin' yuh way int' town, there's somethin' yuh should know —'

'I'm sure there is, Mister Maguire. I'm sure there's a lot I should know, but I've neither the time nor the inclination right now to hear you out. I'm tired, there ain't a bone in my body that ain't screamin' pain – *and*, for God's sake, I need a bath and a proper bed to sleep in! And that's just what I'm goin' to go get myself. Beginnin' now!'

She gathered the remains of the rags that had covered her and threw them defiantly into the brush. 'Shall we go?'

The half-breed took a step to Maguire's side. 'It would be — ' he began.

'Sure,' said Maguire, his gaze tight on Mary Jo, 'go right ahead. I'm sure our friend here will be more than happy to ride alongside of yuh. Just don't go losin' him in yuh haste.' He grunted loudly. 'And try, for God's sake, to steer clear of trouble!'

Mary Jo's eyes flashed. 'I might well say the same for you, Mister Maguire!'

'Just so, ma'am. Just so,' grinned Maguire, but missed nothing of the new glint in the woman's gaze.

Now that, he thought, was a tear if ever he had seen one.

* * *

She could go to hell, and probably would once tied in with Clant Warre, thought Maguire, as he reined the mare to the northern trail and took the strain of the trailed packhorse carrying the body of Stick Grieves.

Go to hell and find her own way back!

He spat angrily into the dirt and tipped the brim of his hat against the lowering afternoon glare. Trouble was, he mused, what sort of mayhem was Mary Jo going to raise in Sentiment when she told her story to Warre?

How would he react? Would he believe her, and if he did how would he deal with Loose Carne? Or had Carne had second thoughts, come round to saving his own skin, and ridden on well clear of the town?

Or maybe he was still around, somewhere in these hills. Could be he figured on finishing Mary Jo in his own good time, sure in the belief that she would head for town. Could be too that he had a notion to take on those riding with her.

Maguire spat again and swung his gaze over the spread of the hill country. Man could hole-up here for days; pick his spot anywhere along the trail for an easy killing; move like a shadow and disappear just as fast. Never seen, never heard.

That would be fitting to Carne's style.

He broke the mare clear of the main track and let her wander into the scrub bordering the treeline. No point in being a sitting target, he figured. He was in no hurry, anyhow, except to rid himself of the company of a stiffening corpse.

He just hoped the half-breed was thinking along similar lines, keeping low, staying hidden, ranging the main trail, save that his 'company' was very much alive and kicking, and doubtless spitting like a boiling cauldron!

That would figure.

There was a silence among the trees as the day's light dimmed and evening closed in. A silence you could hear and listen to, that was broken only by the sounds of yourself and the movements you made.

Maguire was making very few in that last hour before night settled, but he was listening real close for the repeat of a sound that was about as welcome as a preying scorpion. And probably about as friendly.

It was the sound of the scuffing of a wandering mount's hoofs through dry scrub. A mount moving loose, maybe riderless. But no sound of the jangle of tack, no creak of leather. A sound straying aimlessly.

A packhorse, he wondered, one of those

trailed out by the half-breed? If it was, then how come it was straying? How could it have broken free of the 'breed's direction?

Another scuff – somewhere deep in the shadows facing him. Maguire patted the mare's neck to quieten her and peered into the gathering darkness. Wait, he thought, wait, let whatever was out there come to him.

Maybe the horse would pick up the scent of the mare. Maybe it was already watching, sensing danger or seeking safety. On the other hand, maybe it had nosed the drift of a dead body.

Maguire's hand slid to his Colt, his fingers idling softly over the butt. Could be the mount was not so riderless. Fellow might be working things real sly, easing ever closer.

Maguire swallowed and groaned in the pit of his gut as the palomino broke from the shadows and stood facing him, its eyes dark and empty as if in mourning, the body of the half-breed slung across its back like thrown flotsam.

He groaned again at the sight of the bloodstains. Knifed in the back! Loose Carne's doing? Had to be. But where and how, and what, darn it, had happened to Mary Jo?

If Carne had got his hands on her for a second time, she had sure as hell not seen the sun go down on this day.

SIXTEEN

Maguire moved slowly and as best he dared through the long hours of night – and about as dark, he thought, as a funeral procession with no place to bury its dead as he trailed two mounts behind him like hearses, one bearing the body of Stick Grieves, the other of the half-breed.

Somebody was going to pay, and pay real hard, for the death of the 'breed, of that he was certain. But he had no such surge of confidence about the fate of Mary Jo. She was either dead or dying, knifed in the same way as the 'breed. And Loose Carne was now riding safe and easy for Sentiment.

The scores to be settled were sure mounting up!

But, hell, this was all proving some raw deal to finally retire on! It would be a welcome day

when he reined the mare west for Nevada. And
the sooner, he reckoned, the better.

Amen to that!

The dawn came slow and fretful and mist-
filled through the hills, and Maguire figured he
had covered no more than a handful of miles
through that endless, cheerless night. It was
time to hit the main trail again, put some fast
dirt beneath him, and maybe have a first sight of
Sentiment by sundown.

Nothing to be gained now by treading hot
coals; he was too anxious to get to the killing, to
see Carne and Clant Warre go down to his guns,
see the same look in their eyes as had glazed
Stick Grieves's stare when the ghost came home.

But there was something else, something that
was troubling him to the raw. What to do about
the woman?

Damn it, he could hardly leave her – more
likely what remained of her – for the crows to
feed on. Hell, no, that would not be fitting. So
maybe he should go find her body, bury it
decent, put up some sort of marker. She
deserved that much.

It would take time, perhaps most of the day,
and there were no obvious tracks to follow, but if
he figured on the half-breed having held
roughly to the main trail, then it should be
somewhere along the northern tracks that he
would pick up a clue.

He had no other choice.

But an hour's slow trailing through that misty morning drew a blank, and Maguire was all for pushing on to clear the hills and feel the breaking sunlight warm on his back when an almost last, despairing glance to his right showed him the broken branch and the twist of thread hanging from it.

He reined up, peered closer, and reached for it, turning the twist through his fingers.

Blue thread, same colour as the shirt Mary Jo had been wearing when she left. He narrowed his eyes on the surrounding ground: sand and loose stone, no clear footprints or hoof marks, but there had been a disturbance, and not so long back.

His gaze probed the scrub and bush where it thickened on the slopes to the higher reaches. Not a deal there either, but it was all he had. Could be that Mary Jo and the 'breed had sought cover here. Maybe Carne had fired a shot from somewhere up ahead of them. But how come —

Maguire was easing from the saddle when the crack and whine of a Winchester's retort singed hot lead to within a hair-breadth of his shoulder.

Carne!

Darn it, the scumbag had waited for him!

He dived headlong into the scrub, sweat already lifting in his neck, the wisps of mist like ice-fingers over it. The shot had come from somewhere higher, somewhere in the rocky crags where the hill peaks broke clear of the growth. Some climb, he thought, coming to his knees and scanning the range.

But there was nothing for it but to move – and wait for the next shot.

It came with another echoing whine, but now Carne was guessing, trusting to gambler's luck where to place the lead. Maguire risked a quick glance.

No hint of a shape, curl of smoke, glint of light on a barrel. He shifted again, this time to his left to the deeper scrub. Maybe he could crawl through it, easing higher. Maybe . . . .

A third shot, but now far to the right to the space he had just left. Gambler's luck for Maguire! Maybe he had been dealt a better hand than he had figured. But it was short-lived as two more shots panned the scrub.

He waited. Now it was Carne's turn to sweat.

There had been no return of fire from Maguire, and that would be bothering Carne. He had no target, no means of knowing if a shot had gone home; nothing to shoot at until it moved – if he saw it move.

Take a chance, thought Maguire, and began to crawl.

Hell, if Carne caught so much as a flicker of the scrub it would be all over in one well-placed shot. But Maguire's luck was holding as he crawled on, feeling the lift of the slope beneath him, knowing that he was moving higher.

How high to go, he wondered; to the crags themselves, just short of them, and what would happen when the scrub ran out?

He swallowed, paused, listened. Silence.

He needed to force Carne to show himself, draw him from cover. He needed a diversion. But how, with what, pinned down here in a jungle of growth? Maybe it was just a greedy helping of luck he needed, the sort that came only once.

He swallowed again, licked the sweat from his top lip, and squirmed like an ageing snake another slow yard.

And it was in that shift through the clinging dirt that he saw it.

A tangle of gnarled roots had broken clear of the surface to straggle in a twisted mass away to his left and the more open ground of stone and shale. Supposing, he pondered, he could somehow lift those roots just sufficient to release the stones and set them tumbling down the slope, a bit like a miniature avalanche? Might be enough to fool Carne into thinking Maguire was holed-up in that spot. He might raise himself just that shade higher from his cover to get a better view. He might not. But if he did . . . .

Maguire's hand slid over the dirt with all the tension of a paw moving to its last chance of a kill. The grab would have to be sure, the lift decisive. One grab, one lift.

His fingers tightened on the roots, held there for a moment, then lifted upwards with all the strength he could muster.

There was a sudden crack, a moaning split; trickles of dirt that thickened and broadened grew in pace until they were rushing down the slope in twisting rivers. Dust rose in grey lingering clouds; stones shifted, rocks moved. There was an echoing split as a section of the roots broke clear.

Maguire released his hold, slid back in oozing sweat, and came slowly to his knees, his eyes lit like suns on the crags above him.

The dirt and stones were moving faster now, lifting thicker clouds of dust that seemed to hang there on the morning light like shadowed shapes. Maguire raised himself higher, his eyes narrowing, hand on the butt of his Colt.

Had Carne taken the bait; would he show himself?

There were seconds when Maguire thought he had misread the situation, maybe misjudged Carne, more than likely placed himself at greater risk. Hell, surely the sonofabitch was up there somewhere! Had to be.

And then he was.

Dark as night with the day growing behind him; stiff and straight, his gun power levelled in both hands, and even from here the gleam of a killing in his gaze. Only trouble was, he had no target, nothing save the rumbling sounds and the shapeless swirls of dust.

Maguire drew and fired, once, twice, but the shots were wide. Carne swung round, blazing lead over the light like licking flame, forcing Maguire back to the dirt.

Hell, now Carne had the edge!

He would go on firing blind into the scrub, send down a hail of lead that could not miss. Maguire rolled to his right, but the scrub parted with him. Now what? He was a sitting target unless —

The scream hit the hillside like the agonized cry of a strangled hawk.

SEVENTEEN

Maguire did not move, could not, but Carne did – faster than a flicker of sunlight, and he could almost hear the curse that went with it.

Carne spun back to the deeper clefts in the crags, disappeared for a moment, and rose again on the mound of the hillside clutching Mary Jo to him.

'Sonofabitch!' groaned Maguire as he plunged headlong for the cover of a straggling outcrop.

The woman was alive, but maybe that was a mixed blessing for her if Carne intended to use her as a human shield. Would he try making a break for it, dragging Mary Jo with him, or did he plan on shooting it out, with the last bullet for the woman whatever the outcome?

Either way, he still had the fine edge.

'Lay down yuh gun, fella,' called Carne, 'or

she goes. Right now!'

Mary Jo struggled uselessly against the man's grip, her eyes wild with fear, hate, despair, body writhing, limbs splaying. She was far from being out of fight, thought Maguire, but that was making Carne one hell of a difficult target to close on. A misplaced shot might just as easily blow the woman apart as fell Carne.

Maguire licked the sweat from his lips, blinked, took a firmer grip on his Colt, and narrowed his gaze. Every minute added to Carne's advantage – or maybe tried his patience to breaking point against the struggling woman. No point now in facing it out at this distance, Maguire figured. It was time to gamble – one last hand.

He glanced quickly round. There was the weather-gnawed bone of a dead tree higher and to his right. If he could make it as far as that . . . . Darn it, he would have to!

Mary Jo was still struggling as Maguire slid away from the outcrop and headed for the tree under the spitting blaze of gunfire. But he made it, and hugged the shell of the trunk to him as if life itself depended on it.

Hell, it did!

He risked a glance at Carne who was waiting now, sure that Maguire would have to move again. Too right he would. There was no permanent cover here, not unless Maguire could spirit himself to a termite and bury himself in the dead wood.

Time for another gamble. But which way now? He was surrounded by low scrub; fitting enough for a sleeping rattler, but no place for a man. Perhaps he could —

The morning split again to another scream from Mary Jo, but this time she had broken free of Carne's grip, thrown herself forward and was already tumbling into the scrub as Maguire stood aside from the tree.

Carne's attention had shifted, his gun arm lowered to his side as he moved to grab the woman. Now, thought Maguire, it had to be now!

He fired low but straight to spew lead into Carne's left thigh. The man seemed to hang there on the light for a moment like a puppet dangling on broken strings, then fell face-down and slithered down the hillside.

Maguire waited, legs apart straddling the slope, his Colt trained on the body sliding towards him, blood spurting from it in sudden showers.

'You!' moaned Carne as he slid to a halt at Maguire's feet, his face caked with dirt and sweat, hair plastered to his brow, eyes gleaming and bloodshot.

'Yeah, me,' drawled Maguire, easing back the gun-hammer with a click that took the silence by surprise.

'Who – who are yuh!' spluttered Carne.

'Every day of yuh life.'

And then Maguire shot Loose Carne clean between the eyes.

Mary Jo's silence through that next hour said a whole lot as far as Maguire was concerned.

It told him all he needed to know about her pain, the agony of abuse, the way she had been humiliated, her anger and the despair that spilled out of it. She had no need to spell out the details to him. He could see and read every one of them.

But she was sure as hell torn apart to come to admit to the warnings Maguire had given her, and she was in no way resolved whether to still reckon him killer or rate him timely saviour. She would have to settle that, he figured, to her own satisfaction.

So he thought it best to leave her to herself. Maybe there was no place for him right now in her turmoil.

Meantime, he lit a fire, got a head of steam on the pot of fresh coffee, rounded up the packhorses and Mary Jo's mount, and pondered on the strange sight they were going to make when they finally trailed into Sentiment: the living and the dead! Or maybe he should be reckoning when *he* trailed into Sentiment. No telling if Mary Jo was going on. Not, he thought, that she had any place else to go.

But long before that she was going to have to be told and face a brutal home truth concerning 'Uncle Clant'. This was going to be no time for family unity at any price.

It was closing on noon when Mary Jo was tidied up and tending her mount with a more purposeful look in her eyes and a steadier hand. Only then did she speak.

'We never stood a chance,' she murmured as Maguire waited by the embers of the fire. 'The half-breed never saw him. Neither did I, not till it was too late. I thought . . . .' Her words faded. She stared at the fire, and then directly at Maguire. 'Guess you've been right all along. These men were . . . anyhow, it don't matter now, save to say . . . . ' Her shoulders stiffened. 'I'm tryin' to say thanks again, Mister Maguire, and I surely mean it. T'ain't easy, though, for all that I owe you.'

And that, thought Maguire through a grunt, took a mighty lot of doing! 'It's wild country, ma'am,' he said softly. 'Makes for wild men.'

'I see that. Men of all types, I guess.'

Maguire caught the flash in her eyes. 'All types, like yuh say. Trick is to recognize 'em when yuh see 'em. Takes time.'

'But you have learned the trick. Right?'

'The hard way, ma'am. Deal like y'self. It comes with one helluva lot of pain.'

Mary Jo adjusted her hat. 'I've never met a bounty hunter before, much less ridden with one, but I intend to complete this trip alongside him if you're still headin' into Sentiment, that is.' She glanced quickly at the bodies of Grieves, the half-breed and Carne loaded on to the mounts. 'And I guess you are.'

Maguire's boot scuffed out the embers of the fire. 'I am, ma'am,' he said, his gaze settling darkly on her face. 'I always have, 'cus that's where I settle my business.'

Mary Jo frowned. 'You have friends there?'

'No, ma'am, not friends. Just an enemy. The last one.'

The woman's frown deepened. 'Someone you've been followin'? Searchin' for?'

Maguire grunted.

'And you intend to kill him?'

'I do, ma'am, just as soon as I can.'

'Who is he? Some outlaw, a killer?'

'Both of them, ma'am, and a sight more by my reckonin'.'

'And you know him? You've met him?'

'Oh, yes, ma'am, I've surely met him.'

'So who is he?'

Maguire listened to the silence before he spoke the name.

EIGHTEEN

Spinks Carter rose with the rooster most days and took to his rocker on the veranda of his shack on the outskirts of Sentiment just about the time full dawn was clearing the hills.

It was the habit of a lifetime, close on sixty years, man and boy, in the same town, same shack, same rocker and, for the most part, with the same view of the hills and the main trail leading out of them.

Most types had cleared that horizon and passed this way, he reckoned: settlers and their families, wide-eyed miners, slant-eyed gunslingers, whores and tarts, carpet-baggers and lawmen, card-sharps and Bible-thumping men of the cloth – honest folk, cheating folk and just plain lost and lonely folk. The wagon train of humanity.

And this day, he figured, taking his place in the first flush of morning, would be much the same, throwing up its handful of travellers hitting town for the first time, nodding to him as they drew alongside, passing on to whatever it was that drew them. Some would stay, some ride through, some get drunk, some take a woman. Most would be gone come sundown. All would recall Sentiment as just another town on the main trail north. That seemed to Spinks to be the way of the world.

Odd thing was, though, that this day was already feeling different. No explaining it, thought Spinks, rocking gently, listening to familiar creaks, it just had that feeling. Could be something to do with those mist clouds over the hills; sort of spooky, like old ghosts were breathing real deep. Or maybe it was the heavy silence with no one about yet, not even Sledge at the livery, or Jonah cleaning down the saloon.

Could be, of course, that he had over-indulged with that extra helping of pie at supper, or that third finger of whiskey. Maybe he had slept bad. Maybe he had dreamed.

More likely getting just plain old and long in the tooth, he mused, tamping down the baccy for his first pipe of the day. Age set the mind to skittering and figuring a darned sight more than was good for it – and played havoc with the guts!

Even so, there was something different about this morning. Whatever it was had settled in his bones, and he tended to trust them more than most.

But it was another whole hour before Spinks Carter was certain that this morning was different.

He saw the dust cloud in the first real glow of the morning, blurred against the drift of mist when it broke the hill range, then growing like a slow breath and shimmering on the light.

More than one rider and maybe more than two horses, he reckoned. Hard to tell at this distance. But there was no hurry to them, just a steady pace at little more than a walk, and heading clear for Sentiment.

Must have been travelling most of the night. Could be another set of pants-rats drifters, he figured; tired, thirsty, hungry; or maybe more of them filthy scumbags Clant Warre attracted to him whenever he was in town.

Spinks had spat at the prospect. No good had ever come of having Warre around, and if Sheriff Daly was half the man that tin star signalled he should be, he would sure as hell do something about it.

But Daly, like the rest, was plumb scared into cold sweat at so much as the mention of Clant Warre. Snivelling yellow-bellies!

Well, maybe the riders coming in were not

scumbags. Maybe they were ordinary folk, a family, heading north to the timberlands. Steady work for a fellow up there, so he heard tell.

But there was no wagon.

No, definitely no wagon; dust cloud was too thin and spread loose. Riders. Some marshal and a posse on the trail of Warre and his sidekicks? That would be a laugh! Sheriff Daly would be in a three-legged spin at the sight of them – assuming he was stirred enough and sober enough.

Might be an idea to go wake him, just for the hell of it!

Spinks had stopped rocking at this point and come to his feet. But then he had simply stood without moving, not one step, his eyes widening, mouth drying to cinders.

'Hell!' he croaked, and dropped his pipe as the man, the woman, trailed packhorses and three mounts roped with slung dead bodies came clear of the dust cloud and began their slow procession into the still sleeping town of Sentiment.

'Oh, my. Oh, hell!'

Sheriff Logan Daly's guts had been rumbling fit to burst all night. There had been no peace from the ache, not a minute, and now in this dim half-light of a new day, it felt twice as bad.

Worse, it was spreading like some hot wind off the plains, eating into him, every slovenly joint and muscle. Only one thing for it, he thought, stumbling across his office, more of the same darned poison!

Daly had his hand on the near-empty bottle of whiskey when he heard the slow scuff of hoofs through the street dust, a snort, the eerie easing of leather to a rider's weight. Somebody was about early, hellish early for a place like Sentiment where nobody tended to stir till full sun-up.

Must be drifters, he reckoned, leaving the bottle and crossing to the window. Goddamnit, if Clant Warre had brought in more of them stinking gunslinger friends of his . . . . .

He blinked, rubbed a hand over his face, blinked again and was suddenly unaware of the gripe in his guts.

Was he seeing things? Had the whiskey finally sent him chuckle-headed, spooked his mind so bad that he was calling up ghosts? Was he going to the pit of madness? Was he already there?

He stood back from the window and tried best he could to take a hold of the shaking that filled him, that was lifting sweat faster than a flash flood.

Them trailed mounts out there had been loaded with dead bodies – Warre's men; Stick

Grieves and Loose Carne, and that 'breed from the post. Leastways, it had sure looked like them.

He took a deep gulp of stale air, licked his lips, reached for his hat and rolled to the door. If he had been seeing things, then this was the day that preacher fellow could bear witness to him signing the pledge. So be it.

But he had not been seeing things, not by a long shot, and that preacher would have to wait for some other occasion, he thought, as he stood there on the boardwalk and stared into the eyes of a man who looked even then as if death was his business.

'Yuh the sheriff hereabouts?' asked the man. 'I see yuh are, judging by that badge. Good. Then I'm deliverin' the bodies of Stick Grieves and Loose Carne, wanted through three territories, includin' this one, for murder, rape and robbery, and claimin' the bounty due accordin'. There's also a half-breed from the post back there. Carne knifed him. Be obliged if yuh'd arrange a decent burial for him.' The man spat carefully into the dirt. 'Name's Maguire. This here is Miss Mary Jo Goldway from back East. Meantime, be obliged if yuh'd inform Mister Clant Warre as how I'm in town for a while and stayin' at the hotel over there. Reckon he might be interested in a meetin'.' Maguire spat again. 'Sorry to have got yuh up so early.'

Daly wiped the sweat from his face. 'I ain't never heard of these fellas,' he croaked. 'And they ain't wanted here, mister. Yuh got it all wrong. As for Clant Warre — '

'Just tell him, will yuh?' snapped Maguire. 'Now!'

He reined his mount clear of the boardwalk. 'Oh, and by the way, yuh can wire the money care of me at Century, Nevada – when I'm all through with Mister Warre, that is.'

NINETEEN

Mary Jo stared at the man flat on his back on the bed, hat tipped across his face, arms folded, and wondered how deep he was sleeping. Or was he asleep? You would never know with a man like Maguire.

Seemed like he was sleeping, she thought; steady breathing, eyes tight closed. But appearances could fool, and Maguire was a master at fooling, she reckoned. That way he slept good, when he had a mind for it.

She moved from the window of the room at the Trail Hotel and crossed softly to the chair in the shadowed corner. She would watch him, wait her time, then maybe slip away without him knowing, just long enough to do what she knew she had to – damn it, wanted to, if only for the sake of her Pa.

She shivered in spite of the close warmth of the room and winced at the pains and bruises that still gripped her body. When this was over, when Sentiment and Maguire and the whole nightmare were behind her. . . . Would they ever be? Was she going to just walk away from this, all that had happened, all that might still happen, as simple as that? Close it like a book?

Maybe it would have been better if Maguire had told her nothing of Clant Warre, if he had left it, and her, and gone on to do whatever he was set on – kill the man and ride on to Nevada. Kill like he had an instinct for, and enjoyed.

She shivered again.

Well, maybe it was not going to be quite so easy for him this time, not if she could get to Warre first, tell him who she was, talk to him about Pa, urge him to ride out of Sentiment and keep riding.

Go with him if that was necessary.

Damn it, the man, whatever he had become, was her uncle, her blood. She would do what Pa would have wanted. It was her duty to his memory, and nobody, not Maguire, not a whole posse of Maguires, was going to stop her.

She glanced quickly at the man as he stirred in his sleep. How could he sleep like that, she wondered? Did he dream, did he have nightmares? Did nothing trouble him?

She shivered again. Maybe killing was like a

drug; take enough of it and sleep came easy. Well, sleep on, Maguire, she thought, moving silently to the door, putting a hand to the knob.

Sleep on . . . .

Mary Jo slid from the room like a shadow and smiled softly to herself when she was clear of it.

Behind her, on the other side of the door, Maguire opened his eyes and sighed. There she went again, trusting to her darned intuition! That woman sure had one hell of an appetite for trouble, he thought, swinging his legs from the bed. Fellow never got a minute's peace when she was around!

'He still up there? Yuh seen him? Who the hell is he? And who's the woman?'

'Hell, did yuh see them bodies? Never reckoned I'd see the day of them two trussed like turkeys. Nossir!'

'Yuh see the man's eyes? I seen 'em. Real mean. Keen as a hawk's. Bounty hunter. Gotta be.'

'What about Daly? What's he doin'? He goin' to do anythin'? I figure not. Won't lift a finger!'

'Warre will be the one who's takin' on the doin', yuh can bet yuh sweet life on that!'

'And yuh can say that again . . . .'

The crowded bar of the saloon fell silent as the men gathered there drank, smoked and pondered, waiting for the next voice to speculate on the outcome of this strange, eventful day in Sentiment, the likes of which no one could recall, not even Spinks Carter.

'We're goin' down in history, boys. Folk'll talk about this for years. Yuh'll be tellin' yuh grand-kiddies of the day a stranger faced Clant Warre.' Spinks puffed thoughtfully on his pipe. 'Question is: who'll walk away?'

'My money's on Clant,' called one from the far end of the bar. 'Fair and square. There ain't nobody hereabouts faster than Clant Warre. And yuh all seen how fast.'

'I'm with yuh,' called another. 'When Clant rides in from that shack of his at Sand Creek, it'll be all over. First shot. No messin'.'

'I ain't so sure,' came a third voice. 'Yuh don't know who the stranger is. Could be he's a top gun. Mebbe one of them Oregon guns I heard tell of. Now them guns are fast, real fast. They're known for it them parts. Yep, could be he's an Oregon gun.'

'Don't look no Oregon gun to me,' said a tall man, turning his glass in his fingers. 'More like he's one of them backwoods' drifters.'

'But fast,' came the retort. 'Yuh gotta own to that. Yuh seen the evidence, ain't yuh? Fella's gotta be fast to take out Stick Grieves and Loose Carne and still stand breathin'. That figures.'

There was a murmur of agreement.

'But Stick Grieves and Loose Carne weren't no Clant Warre, were they?' said the tall man. 'Nothin' close to him. I seen a man fall to Clant's gun faster than it takes for spit to hit dirt. That fast, I'm tellin' yuh. Them hands of Clant's work like they had the Devil spookin' them. Yuh'll see.'

'Might be a good thing if somebody did take out Warre,' murmured a small man, adjusting his spectacles. Eyes flashed to him and stared in the long silence. 'What I mean is . . . well, he kinda rules everythin' when he's here, don't he? Man can't speak his mind, 'ceptin' to agree with Warre. That ain't right. Can't be. So mebbe we'd all be a darn sight safer and happier if there weren't no Clant Warre here in town.'

'I'd fasten my lip with talk like that,' said the tall man. 'Yuh might get to sayin' yuh last otherwise.'

The small man shrugged. 'I'm only sayin' —'

'He's only sayin' what we're all too scared to say,' growled Spinks. 'Fact is, he's right. Sentiment ain't got no place for a man like Warre, but he's sure as hell layin' claim to it – and we ain't doin' nothin'.'

'It's Daly should be doin' somethin',' said the paunchy storekeeper. 'He should've stood firm first day Warre rode in 'stead of takin' down them Wanted bills.'

'Yeah, and booked his hour with the

undertaker at the same time!' scoffed a man shuffling a pack of cards.

'That ain't the point. Point is —'

'Point's comin' down the street right now,' called a man from the batwings. 'Clant Warre with Daly ridin' alongside him. And Clant don't look in no sorta friendly mood.'

Maguire stood back from the full view of the window and watched the two riders make their slow way down the dusty street.

So there he was once again, he thought, his eyes narrowing. Clant Warre – mean and miserable as ever, just like he had been on that day in the sand. Maguire ran a hand over his ribs. He could still feel the thud of boots against bone, still hear Warre's laugh, see him spitting into the wind.

'Yeah,' he murmured softly, 'and now it's your turn, fella.'

A movement at the far end of the street caught his eye and brought him closer to the window.

'Hell!' he murmured again, this time with a hiss.

That darned woman, walking straight into Warre's path!

TWENTY

Spinks Carter eased his way through the crowded saloon, pushed open the batwings and slipped into the darker shadows of the boardwalk flanking the street.

This morning was taking some strange twists and turns, sure enough, and there was a whole lot not yet clear by a long shot. Just who, for a start, was the woman talking to Warre right there in the middle of the street, and why was he listening to her so intently? More to the point, what in hell's name had a good-looking woman like her – no saloon tart for certain – to say to a scumbag like him? And where was the bounty hunter, and why had she ridden in with a fellow like that?

Spinks glanced at his timepiece. A quarter to noon, and a heap of day still to come. Heck, he

131

thought, just about anything might happen from here on!

He went back to watching the woman. She sure had a lot to say, but Warre was still listening, motionless there on his mount, eyes fixed on the woman as if she were some ghost.

Daly was beginning to fret, glancing anxiously up and down the street, over to the saloon, then at the hotel. He would be sweating like a pig, mused Spinks; all that liquor from last night oozing out of him in one sticky lather. Serve him right!

Hold it, there was a flicker of movement up there at one of the hotel windows. Daly had missed that, and Warre was too busy to notice. There it was again. Had to be the stranger, biding his time.

Had he set up the woman to face Warre? Why? That hardly figured in the way of things. What sort of a sonofabitch bounty hunter was it that sent a woman to open a showdown account?

Spinks frowned and sucked on his empty pipe. All clear at the window now. Fellow had moved, maybe making his way to the street. Would he face Warre right there?

Heck, Warre was dismounting, handing the reins to Daly, taking the woman by the arm, bringing her this way. She sure had some hell of an appeal for him, must have. Clant Warre had never treated a woman decent in his life. Would never know how. Use them and beat them was Warre's way.

Saloon crowd was getting a mite tetchy; fellows beginning to scatter before the shooting started. Lead might be straying real wild before noon, especially if —

'Oh my!' sighed Spinks. Daly had crossed to the hotel and disappeared inside. That might be a wrong move. Should have stayed alongside Warre. Sheriff was in no fit state to go flashing that tin star all high and mighty. Never had been, come to that.

Spinks glanced at his timepiece again. Give Daly five minutes, no more. Meantime, Warre and the woman had reached the boardwalk, waited a moment, still talking deep, then moved to the batwings.

Woman sure looked earnest, like she was telling Warre the story of her life. Some life, judging by the dead-set of Warre's face! She looked kind of pleading too. Maybe she was bargaining for the stranger's life. She was wasting her breath if that was her tack. Warre only ever collected, and always in full!

Where was Daly? No sounds, no movements from the hotel. Maybe the stranger had slipped out the back way. Would hardly take much to give a numbskull like Daly the slip.

Chances were the lawman was still not seeing

straight.

Spinks waited until Warre had led the woman into the saloon before slipping silently after them. Maybe he could ease unnoticed into a corner. Hell, this was no time to go missing out on a showdown with Clant Warre. Not every day Sentiment witnessed a time like this, and somebody had to come out of it to tell the tale as it happened.

Spinks was into his dark corner by the window seconds ahead of Warre and the woman seating themselves at a table.

Warre had a clear sight of the batwings; the woman faced him – and, darn it, she was still talking! But softer now, as if sharing a secret.

Warre was listening close enough between slugs of whiskey from a new bottle, his eyes flicking like anxious flies to the batwings. Looking for Daly? More likely watching for the stranger.

Spinks shifted just enough to glance out of the bar window. Still no movement at the hotel. Maybe Daly's lily-liver had twitched and he had backed off, too scared now to move, trapped between the stranger and Warre. That would figure. Daly had a real talent for getting into a fix, and a better one for coming out on the right side!

Spinks's gaze narrowed on the woman. She was all through with her talking; shoulders slumped, fingering a glass nervously. Warre watched her, maybe summing up all she had said, but with that same flat light in his eyes. Could be he believed whatever story she had told. Maybe he would smooth-talk her for a while – but do not mistake that look, lady. Clant Warre had stayed alive because he always did things his way, no counting the cost, and with as much cheating thrown in as seemed necessary.

And right now he was hog-sick with the killing of his sidekicks. Somebody was going to pay for that, no matter who. Yourself, ma'am, whoever you are, if it suits, thought Spinks.

Hell, this sudden silence was getting spooky. Who was going to make a move?

Warre would be content enough to sit it out and wait for the stranger. But maybe the stranger had other ideas. No telling his style. Some bounty fellows came head-on, guns blazing for the quick kill; others sidled in like a shadow, no sounds, no movement, till it was too late.

But this fellow would have to be fast to take Warre. That, or lucky.

The woman was talking again, real intense, and she had Warre's full attention. What the hell was she saying?

Must be important, even desperate. Do not bargain for your life, lady. There is no going price!

Wait! Warre's gaze had lifted to the batwings. Something was happening out there in the street. Maybe Daly was heading for the saloon. Maybe he had found the stranger, got lucky and taken him.

Hell, maybe it was all over!

No, not yet. Now Warre was on his feet, pulling the woman to his side. She sure looked all-in. Scared too. Seemed like all her talking had been a waste of time. Best thing she could do if she wanted to go on breathing —

Spinks risked a quick glance out of the window.

'Hell!' he murmured on a throat as dry as plains' dust.

The stranger was crossing the street in the full glare of the sun, his shadow like a long black stake ahead of him, fingers circling the butt of his Colt.

And Clant Warre was right here, waiting for him.

TWENTY-ONE

'I'll tell it like it was. Just as it happened 'cus I was right here in the corner of this very saloon two days back, and saw it all. Everythin'. Every last spit-licked detail. Didn't miss a thing. Nossir.'

Spinks Carter leaned back in his chair, puffed reflectively on his pipe for a moment, watched the slow curl of smoke to the rafters, then eased forward again and gazed over the waiting faces in the crowded bar.

'It was like this,' he began slowly. 'A half after noon by my timepiece . . . .

'Sun was full up, high and strong, and yuh could've sliced the air like a side of roasted beef. Stranger stepped clear of the hotel, large as life, real calm, and crossed the street direct to the saloon.

'Mighty slow he came, but no hesitation, and yuh could tell by his eyes what was rattlin' through his mind. Them eyes were dark as night, near black in that steady stare, full of hate for the fella waitin' this side of the batwings.

'Could've heard a fly steppin' out in that silence . . . .

'Warre was on his feet, the woman clutched close at his side. Couldn't figure then where she fitted into all this, but she sure as hell looked scared, like she was full of despair, and she was shakin' somethin' rotten. I reckoned for a moment she might pass clean out, but she hung on there as if time was standin' still and she was kinda lost in it.

'Seemed like an age 'til the stranger reached the boardwalk, and I'll tell yuh straight up I was sweatin' fit to melt! Same went for Warre. Know somethin', I reckon Clant was fair spooked that mornin'. Mebbe it was somethin' the woman had said – and, hell, she'd said plenty! – or mebbe it was Stick and Loose bein' taken out like they had, but whatever, he weren't settled to his usual self. That stranger was gettin' to him, and it showed.'

Spinks puffed thoughtfully on his pipe and watched the glow of the baccy in the bowl. 'Yeah,' he began again, 'gettin' to him. But nothin' happened for a whole minute, like the whole territory hereabouts was sleepin'. There was just silence. Nobody movin'. Nobody breathin'. I recall as how Ben Wilton's two-bit hound howled out somewheres back of the livery – just like it was spillin' a last lament.

'Then came the creak. That was the stranger easin' closer. Warre caught it and stiffened. The woman's mouth dropped open. Thought for a second Clant was goin' to blaze lead there and then, but he had nothin' to fire at, so he just stood there, Colt in one hand, the other keepin' a hold on the woman.

'Yuh could hear the stranger movin' in; soft, steady steps on the boardwalk out there, but he weren't in no hurry for a fast showdown. Nossir. Nothin' hurried. When the shootin' came it was goin' to count.

'But I figured on somethin' else. Mebbe the fella was a whole lot concerned for the woman. Heck, they'd ridden in t'gether, so there had to be somethin' between them. Fella like a bounty hunter don't just pick up a good-lookin' woman in the scrub, does he? He don't go findin' her under some sprung cactus. They must've gotten t'gether somewhere, sometime. God knows how, or for what reason, and I sure as hell couldn't figure why the woman had gone to Warre like she had, but I reckoned on how the stranger had gotta move real careful if he weren't goin' to take out the woman with Clant

– or worse, see Clant take her out.

'And that sorta changed my thinkin'. The fella out there on the boardwalk had a real problem, a joker in his pack – the darned woman! – and Clant Warre knew it. He knew, sure enough, as how there weren't goin' to be no wild shootin', not while ever he had the woman close to him. And yuh can take it from me, he had her close as an undershirt right then.'

There was a long, low murmur of understanding from Spinks's audience before he raised a hand, and continued. 'Next thing I knew, the stranger was at the batwings, clear as day, starin' straight into Warre's eyes. But Clant didn't move, never flinched. Just stood there levellin' his Colt, still holdin' the woman, and she seemed not to believe what was happenin', like she was in a daze, or mebbe seein' the future rush at her faster than a spooked steer.

'Tell yuh somethin', I was swallowin' pure dust when that fella pushed open the batwings and stepped inside.

'Pair of 'em – Warre and the stranger – eyed each other like dogs over a plate of meat, but Warre was lookin' closer, tryin' to see who the fella was, recall his face from some place back, and the stranger let him relish the slow recognition.

'Then the fella spoke. "Remember?" he said, a kinda wry grin comin' to his lips. "Yuh ain't f'gotten, have yuh, Clant?" That's how he said it, cold and measured out like a finger of old whiskey. Yuh could see Warre gulp real deep. He remembered, sure enough. Yessir, he recalled, and he sure as hell didn't fancy whatever it was passin' through his mind. Not one bit he didn't. It was like he was seein' a ghost.'

Spinks paused to examine the bowl of his pipe, tamp the baccy into place and take a long drink from his glass of beer.

'Yeah,' came a voice from the back of the bar, 'what happened then, f'Crissake? Who made the move?'

Spinks replaced the glass and raised his eyes. 'Yuh sound just like Ben Wilton's hound, fella – an interruptin' howl! Yuh gotta flea, then go ahead and scratch it. Otherwise, settle down!'

He waited until the laughter had died, and then went on, 'Hard to say what might have happened then if the woman hadn't been there – if she hadn't moved like she did. But she sure set the rattlers scuttlin', and hell broke out like it had been penned all night. She tried squirmin' clear of Warre's grip, arms and legs twistin' and turnin' and slitherin' like a snake, but Clant held firm with that gun of his trained square on the stranger.

'I figured then the fella would move, take his chance with a shot – he might've got lucky – but he just seemed tied down where he stood, watchin' every shift and turn, eyes flickin' nervy as moths at a candle.

'A chair went skiddin' in the struggle; table rolled over, whiskey sloshed to the floor, but Warre was still holdin' tight to the woman, and she went on squirmin' and spittin' and tryin' to drag Clant deeper into the back of the bar – that dark corner over there by the door. Know what, seemed to me like she was pullin' Warre clear of the stranger's range, tryin' to get him to the door, darn it. Figure that . . . .

'Anyhow, then the fella moved. He stepped real smooth to his right and called out to Warre to let the woman go. Some hope! Warre just grinned that long, sickly grin of his, and tightened his hold on the woman, bringin' her round to the front of him like a shield. Hell, he was goin' to let her take the first of the lead and that's when the stranger changed tactics. Oh, yes . . . yuh could see it in the set of his face, them eyes piercin' the space like they was flame. He went real loose, relaxed. I seen that before in a gunman. It's a kinda way of windin' themselves up – just like he did as he gathered himself, tight as a knot, every muscle thrustin' for all his strength, and lunged across the room in one almighty leap and heave.

'Never seen a fella move so fast – never thought there was a fella had it in him – but he sure had, and it took Warre right off balance. He sure hadn't been expectin' no such reaction and he let rip a shot, high and wild, but nothin' to trouble the stranger. Yuh might've thought he'd never heard it. Next thing there's a whole heap of arms and legs and twistin' bodies all over the floor by the bar there. No tellin' who was on top of who! Just seemed like it was one spittin', gruntin' mass. I was on my feet now, wonderin' what the hell to do, but I stayed tight, right here, when Warre came up dark as night and let rip another shot. Could've been he intended it for the stranger, but it went stray again and caught the woman high on the shoulder and she rolled clear in a spray of blood.

'Yuh can still see the stains if yuh look close.

'That left Warre with open space between himself and the stranger who was still spread out on the floor. No doubt then in my mind, no question of it: one more shot would settle it.

'I wouldn't have given a tin-can for the stranger's life. He'd had it. He could see it. And Clant knew it. Darn it, I was all for closin' my eyes on what was comin'. The stranger first, then the woman – and, f'Crissake, m'self next! There was no way Warre was goin' to leave a livin' soul in this bar. He was in for the kill – and that meant everythin' that moved.'

Spinks paused for another gulp of the beer, waited a moment, listening, it seemed, to the

143

silence.

'But that weren't to be the way of things,' he went on.

'Neither Warre nor the stranger had figured on the woman – and that included me. She had simply rolled away and I reckoned on her bein' clean out. Not so. Nossir! Next thing I knew there was a splinterin' of glass, a yell fit to stir Boot Hill, and Warre was fallin' back like he'd been pole-axed. Would yuh credit it – the woman had reached out for the whiskey bottle and cracked it like a rock across Clant's leg. A dead-eyed aim! No tellin' how she raised the strength, but she did – she surely did.'

'She had guts,' murmured a man.

'Some woman,' added another.

Spinks raised a hand. 'Now yuh can see the picture a deal clearer. That move of the woman's was all the stranger needed, just the edge he'd been lookin' for and waitin' on, and when it came . . . . It took just seconds for his Colt to roar twice and for Clant to have no chance with his gun hand hangin' loose, and then for him to watch them shots comin' his way, like he could see the very line of them; to see his own blood bubblin' out of him sleek as a holed barrel.

'I ain't never seen a fella look like he did before. Death had a hold on him, he could feel it, and there weren't no shruggin' it off or turnin' back – but he just stared for what must've been a whole half-minute, then he frowned just as if he was wonderin' how all this had come about. Next thing he was grinnin', or mebbe tryin' to smile, and he had the woman clear in focus. I'll wager my pants he tried to say somethin' to her, but there weren't no words yuh could cotton to, not a sound that made any sense. A sorta murmurin', then a groan and a moan through his last breath. Seemed to me it echoed an awful long time after.'

Spinks sighed and blinked.

'And that was it. Silence just hung there then like it was fixed in the place and wouldn't never shift. I sorta moved, I suppose, and the stranger looked at me, grunted, and went to the woman. He lifted her in his arms, turned again, and said as how I'd find Sheriff Daly trussed up in the hotel. I was to give Warre a decent burial alongside his sidekicks.

'Mebbe I tried to say somethin', but it never came and all I heard was the fella sayin' he was all through here and was ridin' out, but if I'd seen what happened I was to tell it true and right, no fancy trimmin's, no addin' a mite here, a snitch there. Just as it happened. And that, folks, is what I've done. Told it just as it was. And yuh know somethin' – I been to figurin' since that day, takin' time to see it and kinda reflect. Don't make no sense, but it's fact; that

was all over, life and death, in less time than it
takes for me to down my supper. Now ain't that
somethin to think on?'

TWENTY-TWO

The trail heading west out of Sentiment was a deal lonely, mused Spinks Carter, rocking gently on the veranda of his shack as he watched a new day cleaning out the shadows of night. Or so he had heard said.

Drifters reckoned as how a man could trail for weeks without seeing a soul – sometimes not so much as a flea jumping – and get to wondering if this really was the last page of civilization.

A mite exaggerated, Spinks reckoned, but he took the point. There was a whole country out there still not seen save by Indians, hawks and the buzzing busybodies underfoot. Even so, it had been the stranger's choice when he had finally ridden out of Sentiment.

Heading Nevada way, he had said. A long way to Nevada, thought Spinks. Fellow had to have a good reason for trailing that far – but maybe the stranger had. The woman for one.

Man might trail a whole world for a woman like her, in spite of that strangely scared look in her eyes. Well, she was still young, still learning the ways of things, especially out here where a woman often had to be two-parts gunslinger before she could get to being anything like female.

Still, she had sure hitched herself to a good teacher. Bounty hunter he might have been – might still be – but he had another side to him, Spinks figured. Hard to put a finger straight on it; just that he was not all mean, not all hungry for the prize. Hell, he could shoot, no denying that, and handle himself like a mountain lion – and maybe be just as gentle when the time came.

More likely the right person came along.

Spinks sighed. Well, whatever, he and the woman would be well clear of Sentiment territory by now. He just wished there had been the time to have a closer conversation with the fellow; maybe learn just a shade more about him, and about the woman.

On second thoughts, no chance. Fellow like that was not the type for talking on about himself; and the woman . . . well, she had been in town for a reason, something to do with Clant Warre, that was for certain. But nobody would ever come to know the full story of that.

Not, perhaps, that it mattered a great deal. Pair of them had ridden in, done their business, and ridden out. Simple as that, on the face of it.

Trouble was, things were never *that* simple, not where human beings were concerned. Guess the bounty hunter with the fast guns would know that better than most.

Still, here was a new day coming up clear and fresh, just like yesterday. No, frowned Spinks, not just like yesterday.

There would never be another day like yesterday.

The glow of the firelight reached over the evening gloom like a hand and settled the shadows to softer shapes in the tree patch flanking the open plain. Night was close, but the air was warm and the wind half-sleeping in the easy silence.

'Feelin' better?' asked Maguire, watching Mary Jo where she lay beneath the blanket. 'Wound's lookin' a deal cleaner. Reckon yuh'll be good as new come another day or so.'

Mary Jo stirred and smiled softly. 'Reckon I will at that, thanks to you – again!'

Maguire shrugged. 'Figure the thanks should be comin' from me. Yuh saved my life back there at Sentiment, yuh know that? Wouldn't be here now if yuh hadn't — '

'That's over,' said the woman. 'Over and into the past like a lot of things. There isn't any other way.'

Maguire sighed and stared into the flames. 'Mebbe. Some things go easy. Some don't.'

'Clant Warre, for instance?'

'Him among them.'

'You were right about him, Maguire. He was bad, all bad. Right through. Not my Pa's brother, that's for certain.' Mary Jo's gaze drifted to the high night sky. 'I found that out fast enough, and the hard way. Too hard for me to take at the time, it seemed.' She paused. 'He wouldn't listen to me. Didn't want to neither. Didn't really know me, I guess. It was like time had eaten away at whatever there might have been between us. His family life had gone, just as easy as his memories of Pa. Know what he said, Maguire? He said as how homesteadin' back there at Willadon had been a fool's game, not worth the dirt under a man's boots. That's why he'd left all those years back. He'd reckoned on there bein' an easier way of makin' money. Imagine that, will yuh; how does a fella come to thinkin' that way?'

Maguire prodded a stick at the flames of the fire. 'Man comes to a way of life for many reasons, ma'am, not all of them for the best; some by accident, some he's forced into. Never any real tellin'. But for Clant Warre — '

'It was for all the wrong reasons, I see that now. Only thing I don't see so clear is his reaction to me. I'm as near certain as I've ever been about anythin' that he would have killed me when the time came and he figured it right. Killed me, in cold blood, without a thought for Pa and me bein' his own niece.'

'A darned sight worse than killin' yuh, I'd reckon.' Maguire's gaze darkened. 'Yuh were lucky, ma'am, and that's the truth of it. We were both lucky.'

Mary Jo pulled at the blanket and settled it into her neck. 'Well, maybe, but that ain't the only thing you were right about, is it? You were right about me too. Me in particular. And don't you go protestin' none. You were right, I should never have been out here like I was. Maybe I should never have left Willadon. That was my first mistake. There was a whole heap more right on its tail!'

'So what yuh plannin' now?' asked Maguire. 'Yuh headin' back home? 'Cus if yuh are, ma'am, yuh on the wrong trail. This country heads due west – no other place. But there is a town comin' up – three or four days ride, I'd figure – and I'm sure there'd be a stage run through there that would take yuh back east when yuh good and ready.'

Mary Jo relaxed beneath the blanket. 'Is that so,' she said quietly. 'Well, that might be somethin' real useful for them headin' east, but I don't reckon on it for me.' She glanced at Maguire. 'No, I reckon on keepin' goin', due west, like the trail.'

'And where in tarnation are yuh plannin' on settlin', ma'am? Take it from me, there's – '

'I know what yuh goin' to say, Maguire: there's a whole wild country out there, no fit place for a woman, no place for her to be on her own, too many hazards, too many dangers, 'specially for a woman who ain't got much of a notion of the world. You've said it all before. Remember?'

Maguire sighed. 'All I'm sayin' is —'

'You tryin' to get rid of me now, Maguire? Is that what you're thinkin' on?'

'No, I didn't say that, ma'am. I'd be happy enough to see you to the next town; see yuh safe on a stage . . . . All that, and whatever else yuh get to needin'. But I sure as hell ain't goin' to let yuh — '

'I reckon I might settle on Nevada,' said Mary Jo sharply.

Maguire felt a cold grip on his guts. 'Nevada,' he murmured.

'Nevada – that's right. Same place you're headin'. I don't see any good reason why I shouldn't settle on Nevada, do you? After all, you say you're all through with bounty huntin' – and that's good, I'd go along with it; time you hung up your guns, anyhow. So, if you're plannin' on takin' some place in Nevada, some homestead, I guess, why not let me help you? I know a darn sight more about homesteadin', Maguire, than you've got the time to learn first off. Could be you'll need me. What do you say?'

Maguire stared into the flames and stayed silent.

'And another thing,' added Mary Jo, 'while we're gettin' to wherever it is we're goin', you can start teachin' me a few things about this *"real wild country."* That a deal? Beginnin' in the mornin' . . . .'

Maguire simply stared at the flames. They were a whole lot cooler than his thoughts!

TWENTY-THREE

Spinks Carter reckoned that this day – almost two years to the very hour since the shooting of Clant Warre in the saloon bar – would mark the five-hundredth telling of the tale.

And hell, he thought, taking his seat before the assembled audience of drifters and newcomers to the town of Sentiment, he just never tired of spinning out the yarn! Never had and he guessed he never would. Not that he had changed it a mite in all that time; not one detail. He had always told it 'just like it was'.

So maybe that day and the shooting had become something of a legend, put the town on the map, but the telling had never reduced the audiences none. Nossir – they still came; young and old; men and women; from all walks of life, heading for all manner of futures.

And here he was again – for the five-hundredth time with the same anxious faces fronting him, the same anticipation filling the smoky air.

'I'm tellin' it just as it was . . .' he began.

'Hold it, old-timer,' called a voice from the back of the bar, 'before yuh begin, I reckon there's somethin' yuh should be knowin'.'

Spinks gulped and blinked. What the hell . . . nobody had ever dared interrupt before. Who the devil was the fellow standing there in the shadows? No face he could put a name to.

'That so?' called Spinks. 'And what should I be knowin', mister? Care to spell it out?'

'Sure,' said the man, stepping forward. 'I just ridden into town from out west. Came in this mornin' – close on a week's hard ride from seein' the very man you're about to start tellin' of. The fella they call Maguire. The one who shot Clant Warre. I seen him.'

There was a murmur of amazement, a turning of heads.

'Straight up, no kiddin',' the man continued. 'Thought yuh might be interested in hearin' what I gotta say.'

'Dead right!' came a call.

'Yuh can bet,' came another.

'Tell it fella. We're all ears,' echoed a third.

Spinks puffed anxiously on his pipe. 'Well, I guess there can't be no harm — '

'Let the man tell it,' someone urged.

'Yeah . . .' followed a jostling of voices.

'Thanks,' said the man, reaching the front of the audience. 'I don't wanna spoil nothin' of the actual shootin', yuh understand, but I figured as how — '

'Just tell it, son!' roared a half-drunk drifter.

'Right. So here goes. Well, it was like this . . . I was trailin' east just out of a spick of a town called Century when I hit a patch of real bad weather. Heavy rains and storms fit to bust yuh head. I got to lookin' for somewheres to shelter up for the night when I sees this quiet-lookin' homestead up ahead and reins towards it. Figured I might get a hot meal, some coffee, maybe bed down outback some place. And, sure enough, woman of the spread is real welcoming, and says it'll be no trouble at all to step inside and share supper with her and her man. Fella turns out to be about as pleasant; shade on the silent side, didn't say a deal, but yuh could tell by his eyes that there weren't a deal he missed. Kinda had a way of lookin' everywhere at once. Know what I mean?'

'That's him!' called an excited voice, and was instantly hushed.

'Anyhow, supper's fine and the woman says as how I can use the spare bed in the small room. Right friendly, and real welcome, I can tell yuh. Slept like a hound in soft hay!

'Mornin' comes up a whole lot brighter and I figured on makin' an early start, but the woman insists I take some breakfast first. Didn't need no persuadin'! So then I offers to help the fella with a few chores – wood-choppin' and the like – as a kinda thank-you for his help.

'Woman had just called the pair of us for breakfast when these two riders move in. God knows where they came from; never had a sight of them 'til they were on us. Mean-lookin' critters; no-gooders, I figured straight off. And stinkin' of trail dirt to high heaven! Hell, they were rough – and the fella knew it. I could see it in his eyes minute they settled on the scumbags. His look kinda burned into them, like he was seeing clear through them and into their minds – yeah, and figurin' just what they had there, yuh can bet!

'What happened next is hard in the tellin' – '

'Well, get to it, f'Crissake!' roared the drunk.

'One of the critters pulls a Colt real fast and grins at the fella like he's real lookin' forward to puttin' lead between his eyes. "So we finally got to yuh," he drawls. "The famous fast gun. Maguire – the one who put Clant Warre to dirt". Hell, yuh could've knocked me down with a lickspittle. 'Course, I'd never realised who the fella was, but I sure as hell knew the name and the story surroundin' him.

'Maguire ain't armed, and there ain't goin' to

be no chance of him gettin' within a hair of a gun – and the critter knows it. I figured him – and me – for the big hole right then and there.

'And then the shot comes – spittin' flame, buryin' itself real deep into Maguire's shoulder. He falls. I take a dive, but not before I seen that Colt levelled for a second shot at Maguire. Scumbag couldn't have missed.'

Spinks spilled ash from his pipe.

The drunk belched.

The silence waited.

'But the shot that came didn't come from the Colt. Nossir! Know what – it came from a Winchester, roarin' out over the mornin' from the homestead door. And the woman was handlin' it! She took them two gunslingers in two straight shots – and that's the truth. Just two shots. I ain't never seen Winchester shootin' like it. Never. And she did it calm as a kitten. Don't reckon she so much as blinked. Just fired, like it was instinct; killed the critters, put the rifle aside when she was all done, and went to tend her man.'

'And what about Maguire?' murmured Spinks. 'He alive?'

'Sure he is,' smiled the man. 'Alive and kickin'. Never better. 'Course, he took one helluva shot to that shoulder, and close up at that, and he was real pained for a time. But I didn't figure him for the kinda fella who gives up easy, specially not havin' that woman at his side. She's somethin' else.

'I stayed for a few days helpin' out 'til Maguire was back on his feet. Got to know the woman real well in that time. She was tellin' as how it weren't the first time gunslingers and scumbags had come huntin' down Maguire, tryin' to prove they were faster, smarter. None of 'em got too far with that notion!

'She said as how Maguire had taught her how to handle a gun. Reckoned it was for her own good. And he sure did a fine job! Now they seem settled happy enough on that spread of theirs, raisin' stock, livin' the quiet life.

'Came the day it was time for me to leave, and the woman fixed me up good with tack for the journey and said her farewells. Said as how I'd be welcome anytime at their place. Just to ask for Maguire and his wife, Mary Jo.

'Some story, eh? But that's how it happened. That's how it was. Now yuh can get back to tellin' yuh own tale, old-timer. Guess we're ready now.'

Spinks blinked and leaned back in his chair. 'Well, mebbe later. I reckon this young fella's had the last word for now, ain't he?'